A World of Children's Stories

A World of Children's Stories

Edited by Anne Pellowski
Illustrated by Gloria Ortiz

Friendship Press
New York

Copyright © 1993 by Friendship Press
Editorial Offices:
475 Riverside Drive, New York, NY 10115
Distribution Offices:
P.O. Box 37844, Cincinnati, OH 45222-0844

Manufactured in the United States of America
Printed on recycled paper

Library of Congress Cataloging-in-Publication Data

A World of children's stories / edited by Anne Pellowski : illustrated by
    Gloria Ortiz
         p. cm.
         Summary: A collection of children's stories from various parts of
    the world, with general information on different types of tales and
    brief background on each story.
         ISBN 0-377-00259-3
         1. Tales. 2. Children's stories. [1. Folklore. 2. Short stories.]
    I. Pellowski, Anne. II. Ortiz, Gloria (Gloria Claudia), ill.
    PZ8.1.W873 1993
    398.2—dc20   93-13509
                                                              CIP
                                                              AC

Contents

America South of the Rio Grande

Introduction

Sharing stories is one of the few social activities that humans in all parts of the world seem to enjoy. Try to imagine what it was like when the first humans began to share stories. Did they do so by using an early form of human speech? Or did they tell those first stories by drawing pictures on rocks or cave walls or in the sand? Perhaps they told their early stories by acting them out or miming them. We do not know how the first stories were shared. But we do know that for at least 5,000 years, people have been sharing stories in many different ways.

Ways of Sharing Stories

Sometimes stories are told orally, by a live person, to one or several or many listeners. Such storytellers can be grandparents or parents, aunts or uncles, or family friends or neighbors. Or they can be persons who have had special training to help them remember the stories, so they can pass them on to the next generation. Sometimes they are told by a professionally trained teller, who is paid for the performance.

Before the days of writing and books, it was hard for storytellers to remember hundreds of stories. They invented various memory aids to help them keep the stories alive in their minds. In some parts of the world people used string to help them remember. They twisted it in knots, such as the quipu of the Incas of Peru, or they made a series of pictures by moving the string over and under and around their fingers and hands in tricky maneuvers. If you have ever played the game of Cat's Cradle with a friend, you were sharing the remnants of a string story that was first invented centuries ago.

In other places, people used beads on boards or etched special codes into wooden story boards. Only the storyteller knew what the special patterns and symbols meant. Some of these codes were so secret, they have not been decoded to this very day.

Other peoples used music, because a tune seems to make it easier to remember words. Many ancient stories, such as *The Iliad* and *The Odyssey* in Greece, were sung, not told. In Egypt, there are still singer-tellers who narrate tales in ballad form. Some of these are about a character called Mohammed the Prudent. "The Prince Who Learned a Profession" is retold from such a ballad.

Many African peoples of today continue to use music as an integral part of their storytelling. Sometimes the music is played on special instruments, such as one often called a thumb piano in English. It is not really a piano at all but a special type of instrument, unique to Africa. It has many names in the different African languages, such as *mbira, kalimba, sanza, asologun, kankobela.* Other times the music takes the form of songs that seem, to many North American ears, to interrupt the story line when they are sung by the teller and answered in singing by the audience. But this call-and-response singing is the means some African peoples use to create a special bond of togetherness as they share stories.

In quite a few places in the world, while telling their stories, the people drew pictures in the sand, mud, or snow, or on more permanent surfaces such as bark, rock, cloth, or wood. Among some Inuit (Eskimo) groups, the first plaything a child was given was often a knife! Not a sharp knife for cutting but a storyknife. The children would say to one another, "Let's go storyknifing!" after there had been a fresh snow, and they would go out and draw pictures in the snow with their knives as they told stories. Or they might do it in the mud after the spring thaw.

After writing and printing became common, stories could be recorded and copies could be circulated to many people. Then stories could be shared by reading, either aloud to one or more listeners or silently to oneself. Some of these recorded stories have only words to create pictures in the minds of the readers or listeners. Others have illustrations alongside the words, and then the reader or listener can decide how closely the illustrator has matched what the words say.

Still another means of sharing stories is by having them acted out. Since early times, stories have been presented by live actors, marionettes, or puppets on a stage, in an indoor or outdoor theater. Once photography became widespread in the 20th century, more and more people have been watching and hearing stories presented by actors or animated (cartoon) characters recorded on film or videotape or sent directly over the air by television.

In some parts of the world, where books, film, and television are rare or expensive, stories continue to be shared in the old ways. But even in countries where modern ways of recording are readily available, there are still people who believe a story is better if it is passed on directly by word of mouth, from live person to live person, rather than in some indirect, recorded format.

Kinds of Stories

What kinds of stories did the first humans tell? We know as little about that as we know about *how* they first shared stories. The earliest stories are at least 5,000 years old, because there is either picture evidence or writing on clay tablets or papyrus that tells us a little about them. But they may be much older than that. Starting about 3,000 years ago, we know more about the different kinds of stories that developed because professional tellers kept passing them on orally or writing them down or showing them in picture sequences on cloth, dried leaves, wood, or stone that survived. Many of these stories were told for religious reasons, and religious devotion helped to keep them alive.

Perhaps the most common type of story to be found in all parts of the world is the origin story. Such a story tries to explain where humans, animals, plants, or other parts of the environment came from and why they look and act the way they do. "How Medicine Came to the People," "How the Land Snail Got His Shell," "The Alphabet," and "The Story of Our Fingers" in this collection are origin stories.

Another common type of story is the personal-experience story, in which someone relates an event or series of events that happened to her or that she observed happening to someone near her. Modern stories have often been of this type. When such stories are well written, we feel we really know the person or persons in the story and that we are experiencing the events firsthand. Because humans have always been prone to exaggeration, personal-experience stories sometimes get a bit unbelievable, but their basis is usually real events. Some personal-experience stories in this book are "The Riot," "I Am Forgiven," "Bole Gets Dressed," "Siime's Handkerchief," "The Bad Child," and "The Little Red House."

Repetition makes a story both easier to tell and easier for the listener to remember. Also, in all parts of the world, it is obvious that there are consequences to certain human and animal behavior. These points—repetition and the law of cause and effect—are combined in the cumulative tales that can be found in so many countries. "The House That Jack Built" and "The Old Woman and Her Pig" are two well-known cumulative tales in English. This collection has one of the oldest of all cumulative tales, "The Mouse Bride," from the *Panchatantra* of India, and three examples of more recent cumulative tales: "The Little White Rabbit" from Portugal, "The Naughty Frog" from

Myanmar (Burma), and "The Singing Frog" from Argentina and Venezuela.

Parables and fables are two related types of stories. Both of them are short, and both are meant to teach a moral lesson. Jesus used the parable very effectively, and the parables of the New Testament, such as "The Prodigal Son," remain some of the most widely known stories throughout the world. The fable usually uses animals as characters, but the animals act like humans. The most famous fables in the Western world are those of Aesop, from ancient Greece. Buddhists use a form of teaching story that combines elements of the parable and fable. These stories are called Jatakas, and Buddhists believe they tell about the actions and adventures of the Buddha in his former lives. In this collection, the Thai "I Don't Want to Be a Buffalo" and the Iranian "Mirror Hearts" can be considered modern parables, while "Grasshopper and Toad," from Mali, is a pure fable.

Riddles have had a fascination for young and old for centuries. In some countries, especially in Africa, the storytelling session begins with riddling. Often the riddles are short and pithy, but sometimes they are very poetic and full of metaphor. The Hmong people of Southeast Asia had a form of sung riddling contest that involved the riddler and the audience in a careful observation of the environment. An adapted version of such a game can be found in the selection "At the Edge of the Sky." And there are riddles that extend into full stories, such as "Juan Tonto," from Mexico, in this collection.

Some stories were developed to bring about social change, usually in a light-hearted and amusing way. For example, before the handkerchief was in common use, it was considered quite all right to wipe one's nose on a sleeve or with the fingers of the hand. But gradually, it was considered more polite (and more hygienic) to use a handkerchief. Many parents and grandparents got their children to accept the handkerchief by telling amusing stories, all the while making intriguing figures with it. "The Husband and Wife Who Wanted a Child" is based on such figures. Many of the drawing stories passed on by children in Japan, such as "Rainy Day Drawing Stories," had a partly educational function as well.

Most of us are accustomed to stories with a beginning, a middle, and an end that satisfies us and answers our questions. But some peoples have stories that are very open-ended. They seem to leave us with more questions than before we started the story. Or the events in the story can be explained in several ways, each one equally valid. An example of this type is the dilemma story, in which there are at least two equally plausible responses. "Who Is the Cleverest?," from Zaire, is a well-known dilemma story.

Trickster stories are found in many parts of the world. The trickster can be human or animal but in any case usually represents the deceptive side of natural creatures. In some stories, tricksters use their wiles in order to achieve justice or harmony. But in most stories, they do their tricking simply to get the better of another. Rabbit (or Hare) is one of the best-known tricksters in stories from many parts of Africa. He is known under such names as Zomo or Kalulu. In the Americas, he came to be known as Brer (Brother) Rabbit or, in Spanish, *Tio Conejo* ("Uncle Rabbit"). The rabbit story given in this book, "Brer Rabbit and the Rock Soup," was written down in the United States more than a hundred years ago. Anansi the Spider is a trickster character in many stories from Ghana and nearby areas of West Africa. Most of these stories have specific songs associated with them, as does "How Anansi Spread Wisdom" in this collection.

Finally, there are the stories that seem to be for pure enjoyment. These often combine real people and events with magical characters and events. In such stories (for example, "The Bear and the Three Granddaughters," "Ti-Jean and the White

Cat," "Gammon and the Woman's Tongue Tree," and "Casi Lampu'a Lentemue"), animals can often talk and reason, and humans can sometimes understand animals. Objects sometimes come to life and usually help the hero or heroine, although they occasionally hinder them. Most of us like such stories because they give us the feeling that, although there are many dangers and evils in the world, in the end we are safe, as long as we do the right things, help others, and remain true to ourselves.

Whether you read these stories or tell them or listen to them, I hope you will enjoy all the different types.

Asia East of the Caspian

The Mouse Bride

This story is from the *Panchatantra*, an ancient book of India. *Panchatantra* means "five threads" in Sanskrit. For Hindus and Buddhists, the image of the universe as a woven fabric is quite common. There must be a warp of vertical threads and a woof of horizontal threads. Wholeness can only be achieved by bringing together threads from different directions. The stories in the *Panchatantra*, then, were supposed to be like threads that had been pulled together by the sages of the past and were now being given out to young people to guide them in their daily lives. Many of the stories are widely known in Europe and North America, and the average reader is scarcely aware that their source is this ancient collection. The following story is less well known. It is similar to cumulative tales of Europe, and it may have been an influence in the development of that type of story. But basically, the message of this tale follows closely the Hindu-Buddhist belief that in the end, every creature returns to its essential nature.

On the banks of the Ganges, where the billowing waves are full of pearly foam frothed up by the leaping of fishes, there was once a hermitage full of holy men. They spent their time meditating, chanting, fasting, studying. They drank only the purest of water, and they were lean and gaunt, for they ate only roots, fruits, and water plants. They wore simple loincloths made from bark.

One day, the head of this hermitage was bathing in the Ganges and was just getting ready to rinse out his mouth. In that moment, a hawk flew overhead and dropped a mouse that he had caught in his talons. The mouse landed in the hermit's hand.

When he saw what had happened, he placed the mouse on a banyan leaf, and then once again purified himself in the waters of the Ganges. Then, using his great power, he turned the mouse into a young girl. He took her to his wife, who was childless, and said, "My dear, take this girl as your daughter, and raise her carefully."

And so the girl was brought up, with great love and care, until she was old enough to be married. It was the custom then, as it is now, for marriage to be arranged by the parents, so the mother went to her husband, the hermit, and said: "It is time for you to find a husband for our child."

"You are right," said the hermit, and he quoted many verses from sacred scripture about the correct way to select husbands for girls. "In the end," he said, "the wise person looks for seven things in choosing a spouse for his daughter:

"He should have good family, and youth,
He should always tell the truth;
A good job, some money, and good looks;
And much knowledge of good books."

The holy man then called the Sun. The Sun came quickly and said, "Holy one, why do you call me?"

"Here is my daughter. If she chooses you, I would like you to marry her." He then turned to his daughter and said, "Do you like this great Lighter of the Three Worlds?"

And the daughter replied, "Father, he is too hot. I could not marry him. Call another who is better than he."

So the hermit asked the Sun: "Oh blessed Sun, is there one who is better than you?" And the Sun answered, "There is one who is more powerful than I. It is Cloud, for he can cover me so that I cannot even be seen."

The holy man then summoned the Cloud and said to his daughter, "Daughter, shall I give you this one as a spouse?"

"No," she answered. "He is too dark and cold. Give me someone who is more powerful than he."

The hermit asked the Cloud: "Is there one who is stronger than you?" And the Cloud replied, "The Wind is stronger than I, for he can blow me away or cause me to break up into a thousand pieces."

The holy man called for the Wind and then asked his daughter, "Would you like to take Wind here as your husband?"

"Father, he is too fidgety. Call for someone who is mightier than he."

The holy man asked the Wind, "Who is mightier than you?" The Wind replied, "The Mountain is mightier than I, for when I come up to him he stops me from moving farther."

The hermit pointed to the Mountain and said to his daughter, "Shall I give him to you as a husband?"

"Oh, Father, he is too hard and rough. Please find someone else."

"Who is greater than you, O Mountain?" asked the hermit. And the Mountain answered, "The mice have more power than I do, for they push through me and fill me with holes."

The hermit called a Mouse. "Little daughter, do you like this one for a husband?"

As soon as she saw the Mouse, the girl thought, "He is one of my own kind." A thrill of joy passed through her whole body, so that it made her hair stand up on its ends. "Father, turn me back into a mouse and give him to me as a husband. Then I can keep a household as all of my people do."

And her father, because he had such great power through his holiness, turned her back into a mouse.

Not the Sun, nor the Cloud, not the Wind, nor the
    Mountain
Did the Mouse-girl choose as a spouse, but one of her
    own;
For likeness never likes to go far from likeness.

The Naughty Frog

This traditional cumulative tale uses the question-and-answer format. A more common formula, such as is found in "The Old Woman and Her Pig," from England, is to have the petitioner repeat the entire cycle of requests each time a new thing is asked.

"Tree, Tree, why are you crooked?"
"Because the heron perched on me."
"Heron, Heron, why did you perch on Tree?"
"To watch a fish that rose to the top of the water."
"Fish, Fish, why did you rise to the top of the water?"
"Because the buffalo waded in my pool."
"Buffalo, Buffalo, why did you wade in Fish's pool?"
"Because the herdboy prodded me with his stick."
"Herdboy, Herdboy, why did you prod Buffalo with a stick?"
"Because I was hungry for rice but it wasn't boiled."
"Rice, Rice, why weren't you boiled?"
"Because the fire did not burn."
"Fire, Fire, why didn't you burn?"
"Because the wood was so damp."
"Wood, Wood, why were you damp?"
"Because the rain poured down on me."
"Rain, Rain, why did you pour down?"
"Because the frog called out for me."
"Frog, Frog, why did you call the rain?"
"Because I was thirsty and dry."
"Naughty Frog! Don't you have enough water in the pool under the banyan tree?"

At the Edge of the Sky

Among the Hmong people in their ancient homelands in the mountains of Southeast Asia, it was common to engage in sung riddling contests. One person posed the riddles by looking around in the environment and making up the questions. Another person answered by looking at the same scene and finding corresponding shapes or figures. Both the riddles and the answers used set patterns, generally based on shape, color, texture, or position, and they were sung in a kind of chant.

What round thing is on the upper edge of the sky?
What round thing is at the edge of the river?
What round thing follows the ox in the field?
What round thing is in front of the woman in the yard?

The sun is the round thing on the upper edge of the sky.
The water wheel is the round thing at the edge of the river.
The colter of the plow is the round thing that follows the ox in
     the field.
The basket is the round thing in front of the woman in the
     yard.

What level thing is at the very edge of the sky?
What level thing is at the edge of the river?
What level thing comes before the ox in the field?
What level thing is in front of the woman in the yard?

The horizon is the level thing at the very edge of the sky.
The raft of the ferryman is the level thing at the edge of the
    river.
The earth waiting to be plowed is the level thing before the ox
    in the field.
The hand loom is the level thing in front of the woman in the
    yard.

What straight things are slanting down at the edge of the sky?
What straight thing is poking up at the edge of the river?
What straight thing follows the ox in the field?
What straight things are at the side of the woman in the yard?

The sun's rays are the straight things slanting down at the
        edge of the sky.
The ferryman's pole is the straight thing poking up at the edge
        of the river.
The furrow is the straight thing that follows the ox in the field.
The hemp strands are the straight things at the side of the
        woman in the yard.

What wavery thing is silhouetted against the edge of the sky?
What wavery thing is crossing the river?
What wavery thing is behind the ox in the field?
What wavery thing is in front of the woman in the yard?

The flying bird is the wavery thing silhouetted against the
    edge of the sky.
The rope guiding the ferryman's raft is the wavery thing cross-
    ing the river.
The harness is the wavery thing behind the ox in the field.
The hemp strand on the loom, before it is pulled tight, is the
    wavery thing in front of the woman in the yard.

What rough thing is at the edge of the sky?
What rough thing is at the edge of the river?
What rough thing is behind the ox in the field?
What rough thing is at the side of the woman in the yard?

The black cloud is the rough thing at the edge of the sky.
The water whipped into waves is the rough thing at the edge
of the river.
The warty toad warning of thunderstorms is the rough thing
in the field.
The discarded bark of the hemp is the rough thing at the side
of the woman in the yard.

What zigzag thing flashes across the edge of the sky?
What zigzag thing moves across the river?
What zigzag thing is below the ox in the field?
What zigzag thing is in front of the woman in the yard?

Lightning is the zigzag thing flashing across the edge of the
    sky.
The ferryman's stroke of the pole from side to side is the zig-
    zag thing moving across the river.
The prints of the ox's hooves are the zigzag things in the field.
The shuttle weaving in and out on the loom is the zigzag thing
    in front of the woman in the yard.

What crossed thing is appearing at the edge of the sky?
What crossed thing is nearing the edge of the river?
What crossed thing is following the ox to the edge of the field?
What crossed thing is in the hand of the woman in the yard?

The evening star is the crossed thing appearing at the edge of
the sky.
The rope binding cargo to the raft is the crossed thing near the
edge of the river.
The brace of the plow is the crossed thing following the ox to
the edge of the field.
The scissors is the crossed thing in the hands of the woman in
the yard.

What pointed thing is touching the edge of the sky?
What pointed thing has come to the edge of the river?
What pointed thing has come to the edge of the field?
What pointed thing is awaiting the hand of the woman in the
   yard?

The tip of the new moon is the pointed thing touching the
   edge of the sky.
The tip of the ferryman's pole is the pointed thing at the edge
   of the river.
The share of the plow is the pointed thing at the edge of the
   field.
The embroidery needle is the pointed thing awaiting the hand
   of the woman in the yard.

I Don't Want to Be a Buffalo
By Saisuree Chutikul
Translated by Mom Rajawong Saisingh Siributr

Buddhists believe that one is happiest when one accepts one's place in life and lives it to the fullest. The story of a buffalo searching for *sanuk* ("joy of life" in Thai) helps us to understand this Buddhist principle.

A long time ago, not very far from Khon Kaen, there was a buffalo. It was owned by a farmer and helped him to plow the rice fields.

Although the work was hard and most of the time quite tedious, the buffalo was reasonably happy. He loved the smell of the earth after the rain. He worked hard and served his owner most loyally.

Then one day, as he was rolling in the cool muddy ditch, he suddenly thought to himself that he wanted a better life. He looked around and saw a group of people passing by.

A thought occurred to him: "I don't want to be a buffalo, I want to be a man! I'll go and live like a man, eat like a man, think like a man, work like a man, and have fun like a man. Yes, why not! I'll go and live among them and then perhaps I'll have a more civilized life."

After he had made his decision, he threw off his buffalo being, said goodbye to the farmer, and walked away towards the village. His life as a man had begun.

He ate like a man, slept like a man, talked like a man, walked like a man, dressed like a man, worked like a man, and spent most of his time socializing with men.

After a while, he found out that there was one thing he could not do. He could not have fun like a man—that is to say —he could not feel the total pleasure of fun, smile and laugh like a man, or feel what we call in Thai *sanuk*. However hard he tried, he could not feel *sanuk*. He could not smile; in fact he hadn't smiled even once since he began living like a man.

He saw many doctors. He talked to many people. He even went to see his buffalo friends, but nobody could help him. He simply could not smile.

So one day he thought of his dear friend the monkey and paid him a visit. The monkey danced for his friend, performed many tricks, and made funny faces—faces that had always made people roar with laughter—but the buffalo did not laugh.

The monkey was at his wit's end so he took the buffalo to see the birds, hoping that the song of the birds would gladden the buffalo's heart and make him happy.

The birds tried to perform many spectacular flying stunts from one branch to another, sang in low notes and high notes, imitated strange noises, and sang most sweetly and joyfully, but the buffalo did not even smile.

The birds did not know what to do, so they took the buffalo to see the worm. When they arrived the worm thought the birds had come to eat him and he tried to hide himself. The birds called out, "Don't go away, Worm! We've come to ask for your help. Our buffalo friend here hasn't been able to smile for months. It's a very serious situation. Please help him."

The worm said, "All right, but Buffalo, you must do exactly as I tell you and don't ask too many questions!" The buffalo agreed.

The worm told the buffalo to follow him but said that it would take them a rather long time as he was able to move only very slowly.

And, yes, it did. It took them nearly the whole day.

The worm led the buffalo and the birds to a large ditch.

He crept slowly until he had nearly reached the water. The buffalo followed until his legs were in the soft mud.

He suddenly had a strange feeling. The mud was cool. The water that reached his feet was wondrously cool. The buffalo walked farther into the ditch where the water was deeper.

He sank into the water and rolled in the mud. He did not care if his clothes got dirty or his face was splashed with mud. He rolled about until he was muddy all over.

"Isn't this wonderful!

Isn't this fun!

Isn't this *sanuk*!"

He shouted with joy. He laughed and laughed until he was quite out of breath. The monkey, the birds, and the worm laughed with him. Then they called out to the buffalo to go home.

"Home? What home?" the buffalo asked. He went on very proudly, "My home is here, my home is right here!"

The buffalo then got up to eat the grass by the ditch. He had never felt so happy and content before in all his life.

The Rabbit and the Moon
By Onchuma Yuthavong
Translated by Mom Rajawong Saisingh Siributr

In Thailand and other Asian countries, the moon shows a face different from the one we see in North America. Many Asians see a rabbit in the moon, instead of a human face. There is a Buddhist story of great tenderness and sacrifice, telling how the rabbit got to the moon. That story helps to explain why the child in this prose poem wants to give the rabbit a gift.

One night Rabbit set out to view the Moon.
He crossed the river.
He climbed over many mountains,
till he came near the moon.
He sat and waited in silence for a while.
Then he thought that maybe the Moon wanted him to speak
first.
"Good Evening, " Rabbit said.
"Good Evening," the Moon answered.
"How do you do?" Rabbit said.
"How do you do?" the Moon answered.
Rabbit thought it would be nice
to give the Moon a birthday present.
He climbed back over the many mountains
and crossed the river again.
He went to town to buy a hat for the Moon.
That night he crossed the river,
climbed over many mountains
and came to the same place.

He gently placed the hat over the top of a tree
and waited all night
till the Moon slowly rose up
to where the hat had been placed.
"It fits him perfectly," Rabbit thought.
"Happy Birthday," Rabbit said.
"Happy Birthday," the Moon answered.
Rabbit happily came home
after climbing many mountains
and crossing the stream.
That morning,
a strong wind blew
and blew the hat
all the way from the tree top
to Rabbit's house.
Rabbit saw the hat and said,
"Mr. Moon also gave me a hat for a birthday present."
Rabbit was overjoyed.
"Happy Birthday, Mr. Moon!"

Rainy Day Drawing Stories

Drawing stories can be found in many parts of the world, but Japanese children have one of the strongest traditions of telling and passing on such stories. There are hundreds of them and each has several commonly known versions. Most often, the words are given in a little song, timed just right so the final figure in the drawing appears at the same moment that the word for the figure comes out of the teller's lips. Exact translations of any of the versions into English would not be very tellable so I have substituted my own words, using only a few of the basic terms from the original Japanese. Numbers indicate when each part of the figure is drawn.

Once there was a mountain. (1)
To the east of the mountain
there were the houses of a
village. (2)
In the fields below the mountain the villagers planted many
vegetables. They planted rows
of radishes, (3)
lettuce, (4)
and carrots, (5)
and in between those rows
they planted rows of
potatoes. (6)
Past the fields there were two
ponds: a round one (7)
and an oval one. (8)
Oh! The pond is overflowing.
Don't let the fish get away. (9)

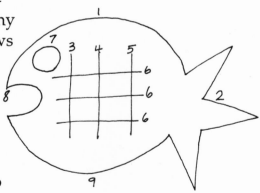

One day it started to rain.
It rained (1)
and rained (2)
and rained (3)
and rained. (4)
It rained so hard that puddles
started to form. (5)
It rained more and the puddles
overflowed and made a big
puddle. (6)
Then it began to rain over
here (7)
and the puddle grew into a
small lake. (8)
Eeeee! (9)
Watch out for the pig! He'll get
you all muddy.

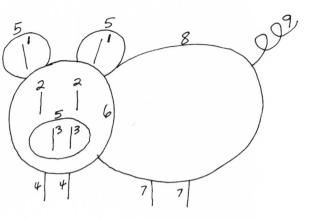

 iddle East

The Alphabet
Retold by Louis Ginzberg

Jewish people are often referred to as "People of the Book." Writing was and is considered very important in their culture. So it is not surprising that the letters of their alphabet should be personified in their legends as thinking, acting creatures. This version of the origin of the alphabet was reconstructed by Louis Ginzberg from ancient sources.

When God was about to create the world by His word, the 22 letters of the alphabet descended from the crown of God, where they had been engraved with a pen of flaming fire. They stood round about God, and one after the other spoke and begged, "Create the world through me!"

After the claims of all the other letters had been disposed of, Bet stepped before the Holy One (Blessed be He) and pleaded before Him: "O Lord of the World! May it be your will to create the world through me, seeing that all the dwellers in the world give praise daily unto you through me, when they say: "Blessed be the Lord forever. Amen and Amen."

The Holy One (Blessed be He) at once granted the petition of the letter Bet, saying, "Blessed be the one that comes in the name of the Lord." And the Holy One created the world through Bet. And that is why the first word in the Bible is "Beh-resh-eet," meaning "In the beginning."

The only letter that refrained from pressing its claims was the modest Alef, and God rewarded it later for its humility by giving it the first place in the listing of all the letters, the alef-bet, the alphabet.

The Prince Who Learned a Profession

This legend is only a small part of a long cycle of tales centered on the character known as Mohammed the Prudent. There are many variants and they are often sung as ballads as well as being told in oral story form.

There was once a ruler who had a son named Mohammed. In his later life he was called The Prudent and here is one of the reasons why.

One day Mohammed said to his father, "I wish to marry."

"Very well," said his father. "I will send your mother to find a girl who is suitable for you."

"Oh, no," said Mohammed, "I want to find her myself." So Mohammed set off on his horse toward the west. He traveled two days and on the third day he came upon a big field of leeks. There was a man digging the leeks and next to him stood his daughter, weaving them in bunches. Mohammed sat down near them and watched them for a while.

"Would you please bring me a drink of water?" asked Mohammed. The girl brought him some water and Mohammed drank deeply. The girl pleased him, and he could see that she was interested in him. So Mohammed called to her father: "I would like to marry your daughter. Are you in agreement?"

The father saw that his daughter liked the idea, so he agreed to the courtship. Mohammed bought a piece of land near their field of leeks, and there he ordered a palace to be built. It was very much like the one his father owned. After it was furnished, he said to the girl and her father: "Stay here in this palace while I go back to my family. I must prepare many things for the marriage. I will return as soon as I can."

Mohammed returned to his father and said, "I have found the girl I wish to marry."

"Who is she?" asked his father.

"She is the daughter of the sultan of leeks."

"Is there really a sultan of leeks?" asked his father.

"There are leeks surrounding the palace they live in; when I left the place and asked someone who lived there he said it belonged to the sultan of leeks."

"Very well," said his father. "Your mother will go and make arrangements for the marriage." So his mother went off, and when she came to the palace where the girl now lived with her father, she said to the girl, "I am here to make arrangements for your marriage to my son."

"What do you mean, your son?" asked the girl.

"My son. The one who came here before. He is the son of a king."

"Oh, I did not know that," said the girl. "Well, if he is the son of a king, I cannot marry him."

"Why not?"

"Because the man I marry must have a profession. He must be able to work with his hands," said the girl.

So the mother returned to her husband, the king, and said, "She will only marry a man who has a profession, one who can work with his hands."

The king sent for the heads of his guilds. He called the first, who was a carpenter, the head builder for his estates. "How long would it take you to teach your profession to my son?" he asked.

"At least two years," answered the carpenter.

The king turned to the head blacksmith. "How long would it take you to teach your profession to my son?" he asked.

"At least a year," answered the blacksmith.

Then the king noticed a man at the back of the group. He was jumping up and down. "Why are you jumping up and down like that?" asked the king.

"I wanted to get your attention," said the man. "I am a weaver of silk. I was once the head of all your weavers, but I wove so quickly and so well that the other weavers pushed me aside. When I heard that you wished to have the heads of each of the professional guilds come, I decided to stand at the back to find out what it was all about."

"Very well, said the king. "How long would it take you to teach your profession to my son?"

"I can teach him in five minutes," said the weaver.

"Are you crazy? How can you possibly teach him in five minutes?" asked the king.

"Send for some silk thread in different colors, and a loom, and you will see if I can teach him in five minutes or not."

So the king sent for a loom and for the finest silk thread and set them in front of the weaver. The weaver turned to Mohammed and said, "I am not going to go into long explanations, telling you to do this or do that. Instead, I want you to look closely and watch exactly what I do with my hands and with the loom and the thread." With his nimble fingers, the weaver moved the silk threads back and forth over the loom, creating a beautiful piece of cloth that showed the king's palace in the design.

"Come, now it is your turn. Make a piece of cloth just like this one," said the weaver. Mohammed took his place in front of the loom. He moved his fingers exactly like the weaver, twisting the silk threads in and out in the same way. In five minutes, he had woven a short strip of cloth. The king left them at work.

Some time later the weaver went to the king carrying two pieces of cloth. "I wove one of the pieces and the other was woven by Mohammed. Can you tell the difference?"

The king had to admit it was hard to tell them apart. He made the weaver his head sheik, to govern over all the other sheiks. Then he called his wife and said, "Our son is now a weaver of silk."

His wife returned to the daughter of the sultan of leeks and said, "My son is a prince, but he is also a weaver of silk. Here is a piece of cloth he has woven."

The girl looked at it and saw it was well done. "Now I will marry him," she said. They made the marriage contracts and celebrated the wedding. Then they returned to the palace the prince had built and began to live happily together. Every day the prince practiced and perfected his weaving, until he became the finest weaver in the country.

He liked to go out, disguised as a simple weaver, to buy silk thread at the markets. One day he was on a search for new thread in a faraway town, when a man standing in front of a house stopped him. "Please come in and share some coffee with me," said the man. "Perhaps I can help you find what you are looking for."

The weaver prince went in, and they passed through a door. It led only to a small room with another door. They opened it and it led to another room with a door. They continued on until they had passed through seven doors, and suddenly the prince was thrust into a room, the seventh door was locked behind him, and he found himself among a group of strangers. "Who are you?" asked the prince. "What are you doing here?"

"We are awaiting our fate," said the others. The man who brought you in here is a poisoner and extortioner. He puts poison in our food and drink. Then he hangs us over a boiling cauldron and threatens to lower us in unless we pay him. He says it is the only way to get rid of the poison. Each time he says he will let us go free, but then he starts the poisoning again."

After two days, the prince had indeed been poisoned and the man came for him and took him to the boiling cauldron. The prince was weak but not so weak he could not think. "How much do you need to get the poison out of me?" he asked the poisoner.

"Oh, at least 25 piasters," replied the man, for he knew that was the amount of money the prince had in his pocket.

"I have something here that will bring you much more," said the prince. "I am a master weaver, and I have here a piece of the finest silk that I wove. I intended to sell it to the prince. If you take it and sell it to someone at court, I am sure they will pay you at least a thousand piasters." The prince brought out a piece of silk in which he had woven the royal design.

The poisoner took the piece of silk to the marketplace and offered it for sale for a thousand piasters. Everyone around began to admire the beautiful piece of silk. Now the prince had been absent from the palace for three days, and his assistants suspected something had gone wrong; so they had gone out looking for him. Two of them were in the crowd looking at the piece of silk.

"Who made that piece of silk?" they asked. "It appears to be by the finest weaver. We wish to commission a piece of work like that."

"Oh," said the poisoner. "The weaver is at my house. I invited him in for coffee and he took ill. You may come in a few days' time and he will be ready to work for you." And the poisoner slunk off with his thousand piasters.

When the king was informed that his son was probably being held prisoner, he came with his soldiers to the house of the poisoner. There he found the prince, still very ill from the poison. When they had freed all the other prisoners, and taken the poisoner to his judgment, the king turned to his son and said, "How wise your wife is. She was right to insist that you have a profession. For it was the work of your own hands that saved you."

Mirror Hearts
By H. Moradi Kermani
Translated by Nouchine Ansari

The author indicated that he did not wish to bring this story to a finish but rather wanted each listener or reader to decide what happened at the end.

There was once a little girl whose parents had died. She was very poor. All that her mother had left her was a mirror. She had to work very hard taking the sheep to pasture, milking, fetching water from the spring, baking bread, and doing many other tasks.

So she had no time to talk to other children or to play with them. It was her imagination that took her away. She made up stories about everything she saw: mountains, stars, springs, cows, people. But she never told her stories to anyone.

One day she met a Gypsy. That wise woman saw the little girl's wandering gaze and her pale face. She knew that the little girl stored many unsaid things in her heart and that this heavy burden would soon break her.

The Gypsy said, "Take a piece of dough from your daily bread and make little people, and tell them your stories."

From then on, the little girl did just that. And every day she broke a piece off her mirror and put a small fragment on each bread figure she made, in the place where the heart should be. So when she told her stories to the little bread people, she saw herself in the mirror bits.

In time, her tales became longer. She needed more dough.

Her portion of daily bread to eat became thinner, like herself. But she felt happier.

Now one day, as soon as she fell asleep, her little people, filled with stories, began to move around.

Abou Hadaba
By Rima Khalifeh
Translated by Julinda Abu Nasr
and Anne Pellowski

The rhyme in this story is part of a longer, traditional one. The author used the rhyme as the basis for a story written in a folk tale mode. The nonsense words and the name Balkis are given as they are pronounced.

Once in an old village in Lebanon there lived a man with a hump. The people called him Abou Hadaba, "Father with the Hump." When he walked by, they would often give him strange looks or glance the other way. Abou Hadaba searched and searched to see if he could find someone else who had a hump like his, but he found no one who looked as he did. He felt different, and unhappy.

One day he said to himself, "I wish I could go to a village where everyone had a hump like mine. But I guess the only place would be the desert, where the camels live. They have a hump like me." But he knew that would be impossible. He had no way to live alone in the desert. Abou Hadaba climbed up and down mountains, walked through valleys, and wandered into many forests, searching for someplace where he could be peaceful and happy.

One day, he was deep in the middle of a forest where he had never gone before. He felt tired and stopped to rest. Suddenly, from the distance, he heard music. "Who is that?" he wondered. "What strange music to hear in the middle of the forest!"

He walked farther into the trees, looking left and right. Before long he could hear the words that were being sung to the music:

> Heess, beess, fill the bag with treats;
> Get some sugar; make some sweets,
> For the little girl, Balkeess.

He moved closer to the spot where the music came from, but he kept himself hidden behind a tree. He saw a group of dwarfs. They were dressed in blue or orange or purple. All of them were busy. Some were measuring sugar, others were measuring flour; a few of them were kneading dough that had already been mixed. All of them were singing.

> Heess, beess, fill the bag with treats;
> Get some sugar, make some sweets,
> For the little girl, Balkeess.

Abou Hadaba knew the words to the rhyme. He could not help himself. He added a line, "On Thursday, Friday, and on feasts."

Astonished, the dwarfs looked up from their work. They saw Abou Hadaba hiding behind the tree and ran to surround him. "How did you get here? Who are you?" they asked.

Abou Hadaba sat down and told them his story and why he had left his village. "I was looking for people like myself, who won't make fun of me," he said at last.

"Don't be sad about your hump, or because you are different," said one of the dwarfs. "We are different, too. But we have learned not to be bothered by our looks. We try to stay happy, by keeping busy and singing and dancing while we work."

Abou Hadaba thought carefully and then he said, "Teach me to sing and dance like you. Perhaps it will help me to forget my hump."

"From the way you finished off that song, you seem to catch on to our music," said one of the dwarfs. "But if you stay with us, you must realize that we work hard, and you would have to work right alongside us. If you are a willing worker, we will teach you our music, as well as how we make our sweets."

Abou Hadaba decided to stay with them. He learned to bake cakes and make sweets and candies of all kinds. And he learned to sing and dance. Every evening he practiced with the dwarfs. He learned many songs, but his favorite remained

Heess, beess, fill the bag with treats;
Get some sugar, make some sweets,
For the little girl, Balkeess,
On Thursday, Friday, and on feasts.

One night he dreamed he was in his old village. In his dream he saw the children from his neighborhood; but they were not teasing him, they were asking, "Where is Abou Hadaba? We have not seen him for a long time." He awoke from his dream and said to himself, "Perhaps it means it is time for me to go back. I will go!"

The next day he told the dwarfs of his decision. They begged him to stay a bit longer, but Abou Hadaba felt compelled to go. "It is as though the children are calling me," he said to them.

So he returned to his village and set up a sweet shop. Often he would walk through the streets, singing and dancing and playing a pair of cymbals. Not only the children but many adults came to see and hear him. Soon the children knew all of his funny songs and dances. They would visit him in his sweet shop. He even taught them how to make certain candies and sweet desserts. But always, he showed them how important it was to sing while they worked. Best of all, they loved to sing the song

Heess, beess, fill the bag with treats;
Get some sugar, make some sweets,
For the little girl, Balkeess,
On Thursday, Friday, and some feasts.

The children no longer called him Abou Hadaba, "Father with the Hump." They called him Abou Sounoozh, "Father with the Cymbals."

But Abou Sounoozh did not forget his friends the dwarfs. From time to time, he went back to visit them. Each time he would learn how to make new and different sweets. And they taught him new songs. But his favorite song was still the one he had heard them singing when he discovered them, deep in the forest.

Heess, beess, fill the bag with treats;
Get some sugar, make some sweets,
For the little girl, Balkeess,
On Thursday, Friday, and on feasts.

Africa
South of the Sahara

Bole Gets Dressed
By Anne Pellowski

In Swahili and many other African languages, specific words for color are not abstract terms. Instead, the names of things (or parts of things) from the natural surroundings that are a particular color are used to describe other things of that color. This is also true, to a certain extent, of terms used for size, shape, sounds. During a children's book workshop in Kenya, the participants began talking about the difficulties this use of language poses for the writers and illustrators in modern-day Africa who wish to create concept books for young children that can help them understand and make sense of the colors, sizes, shapes, and other facets of their changing environment. I was inspired by the discussion to create this story, and I put it into a felt-board format, so that it could be shared in many languages. Each person could adapt the figure and the objects to match the particular terms used in his or her language. The girl is named Bole in honor of Asenath Bole Odaga, the children's book writer and publisher who organized the workshop.

One morning, Bole got up and put on her snowflake underwear! Was it made out of snowflakes? No! it was the color of snowflakes. In English, we say—white.

She put on her banana blouse! Was it made of bananas? No! It was the color of bananas. In English we say—yellow.

She put on her apple skirt! Was it made of an apple? No! It was the color of an apple. In English we say—red.

She put on her mamba snake belt! Was it made of a mamba snake? No! It was the color of a mamba snake. In English we say—green.

She put on her mouse socks! Were her socks made of mice? No, they were the color of mice. In English we say—gray.

She put on her turtle shoes! Were her shoes made of turtles? No, they were the color of turtles. In English we say—tan.

She put on her flamingo hair bow! Was it made of a flamingo? No, it was the color of a flamingo. In English we say—pink.

She put on her bougainvillea flower sweater. Was it made of a bougainvillea flower? No, it was the color of a bougainvillea flower. In English we say—purple.

She put on her tropical bird coat! Was it made of a tropical bird? No, it was the color of a tropical bird. In English we say—blue.

She put on her orange gloves. Were they made of oranges? No, they were the color of oranges. And in English we say—orange!

Now Bole was dressed warmly. She was ready to go with her class on an outing. They were going on a bus up to Mount Kenya, one of the few places in her country where you can see snow.

The Riot
By Wale Okediran

In many parts of the world, when people of different religions live near one another, there are often misunderstandings and strife. The writer of this story wished to point out that it is often children who see the way to accepting others with different beliefs.

One hot afternoon after school, eight-year-old Mary and her elder brother, Samuel, were playing a game of Snakes and Ladders in the family sitting room. Sitting next to his children in his favorite chair, Mr. John Bature was reading the day's newspaper. Suddenly he exclaimed, "Oh, no! Not again!"

Mary looked up. "What is it, Daddy?" she asked.

"It says here that the Muslims and Christians are fighting again in Kano, Bauchi, and Kaduna and that many Christians have lost their property and homes during the riot."

"I hope they didn't kill anybody," said Samuel.

"Several Christians were killed," his father sadly replied. "The riot has also reached Zaria," he added.

The news frightened Mary. "Daddy, won't the Muslims come and fight us here?"

"No, my dear, the riots won't get here. We have more Christians than Muslims here in Kafanchan. The Muslims won't dare fight us."

That Friday afternoon, however, when Mary and her friend Arike were going home after school, they noticed small groups of Muslims in their white *galabiyas* (tunics) and skull caps arguing at street corners in loud voices.

"What are they talking about?" Mary asked Arike.

"Maybe they are just discussing what they heard today at the mosque," Arike replied.

Unknown to the two girls, the crowd was preparing to start a riot. Despite their smaller number in the town, the Muslims were planning to attack the Christians, as their leaders had ordered. In no time, the town's Muslims had poured into the streets chanting war songs. Before long, several churches, shops, and houses belonging to Christians had either been set on fire or looted and destroyed.

As the riot continued, the streets were filled with smoke and the cries of the wounded and the dying. Unable to find their way home in all the confusion, Mary and Arike started crying.

"Help us, somebody please help us," Arike sobbed as the smoke from the burning houses stung their eyes.

"What shall we do? How shall we get home today?" Mary cried. "Please help us, God."

Suddenly they saw some people who were obviously Christians running past them in the direction of the police station. "Let's follow them," Arike shouted, pulling her friend by the hand. As the girls ran, Mary hit her foot against a stone and fell.

"Arike, Arike, please help me," she cried. Arike ran back and pulled her up. By the time they got to the small police station, the place was already full and the girls had to squeeze themselves among the crowd.

A few minutes later, there was a loud noise from the direction of the market as a new group of armed men took to the streets shouting and running after the Muslims in their *galabiyas*. "The Christians are fighting back," somebody shouted. Some of those inside the police station burst into cheers. A few of the youths ran out to join those on the streets who had now started burning mosques and houses belonging to Muslims. As Mary and Arike were wondering what to do, Mary saw the

elderly woman who sold fruits at the shop near her parents' house. She, too, was hiding at the station.

When the sounds of the rioting had faded off into another direction, Mary went up to the old woman and asked, "Would you run with me and Arike to my house?"

The woman agreed to try and they all three raced and dodged to Mary's house. Mary's parents were overjoyed. "We had searched everywhere for you," Mrs. Bature sobbed. "Thank God you're safe."

Then Mr. Bature noticed Arike. "Who is this?" he asked.

"She's my friend, Arike. She sits next to me in class," Mary replied. "Her house is far away so I thought she could stay here until everything is clear."

"Where do you live?" Mrs. Bature asked Arike.

"In the staff quarters of Muslim High School," answered Arike. "My parents are teachers there."

"Then you must be a Muslim," Mrs. Bature said.

"Yes, Mummy, she is a Muslim but a very good girl." Mary interrupted, trying to help her friend.

"I'm sorry, Mary, but Arike can't stay here."

"But, Mummy, she's good and she's my friend. She even helped me when I fell while we were running."

"And I say she's a Muslim and that's bad. If they find her with us they might think we kidnapped her. Don't forget that the Christians have started fighting back. If they discover we are protecting Arike we would be in trouble."

"Please, Mummy, please let her stay," Mary begged.

Arike also knelt down begging, "Please, Ma, let me stay, Ma. My house is very far away and they're still fighting in the streets. Don't let them kill me."

"Hmmm . . . . That's true. Muslim High School is really far away. I wonder if we could. . . " Mrs. Bature started to agree, but she was cut short by her husband.

"No, no, no, she's a Muslim. She has to go."

"We can't keep her in the house," Samuel added. "Muslims are wicked. They are our enemies."

"But Samuel, Mummy, Daddy," protested Mary. "In Sunday school our teacher told us that we Christians should love our enemies. And also that we should help anyone who is in trouble."

"No, my dear," Mr. Bature said, shaking his head vigorously. "That girl can't stay here. It's too dangerous."

So it was that with tears streaming down her face, Arike was turned away from Mary's house. The sight of her friend being sent away crying was too much for Mary, and she too broke into tears. As Samuel pushed the reluctant Arike toward the door, an idea suddenly came to Mary.

"Wait, Samuel," she said. "Let me take my book out of her bag." While pretending to remove a book from Arike's bag, Mary whispered to her, "Go to the back door. I'll come and open it for you."

As the Batures' front door closed behind Arike, she was left alone in the street, which by then had grown dark except for the distant lights of burning buildings. The harmattan wind had started blowing and it was very cold. Arike's teeth chattered from fright and the cold. She quickly crept around to the back of the house and hid behind a hibiscus shrub. It seemed like a long, long time before Mary silently opened the kitchen door and let her in. Mary then quietly took Arike to her room, where she hid her under her bed until her parents went to bed.

The following morning while the Bature family was listening to the news on the radio, the announcer mentioned that Muslim High School was among the places completely burnt down during the riots. He added that some of the students and teachers were wounded and killed. Suddenly, Mrs. Bature remembered that Mary's friend Arike lived at the Muslim High School with her parents. "Poor Arike, only God knows what has happened to her."

Mrs. Bature turned to her husband and told him, "I wanted to keep her here, but you refused. That was not Christian-like."

Mr. Bature looked guilty for a moment, then said, "I'm sure she's safe somewhere. Her parents too. I feel it in my bones," he added hopefully.

Mrs. Bature looked worried. She turned to her daughter and said, "Mary, we're sincerely sorry about your friend. It's possible they escaped. Not everybody gets killed in the riots. All the same, I am sorry we turned her away."

But Mary said cheerfully, "Arike is very safe. I only hope her mummy and daddy are safe, too."

When her parents looked baffled, she added, "Last night when I pretended to take my book from her bag I asked Arike to meet me at the back of the house. Later, I let her in, took her to my bedroom, and hid her under my bed till you went to bed."

"Is she still in your bedroom?" her mother asked in astonishment.

"Yes, Mummy."

"Go and bring her and we'll all have breakfast together." Her father added, "Then we'll go and look for her parents, but don't tell her about the radio news. There's no need to worry her unnecessarily." He switched off the radio as Mary ran to her room to fetch Arike. She soon came back with her friend, who looked tired and untidy from hiding under the bed. As the two girls entered the sitting room, both Mr. and Mrs. Bature ran up to Arike and hugged her. "We are so glad to see you're safe," Mrs. Bature said. "We are sorry we turned you out last night."

"Yes, we are really sorry," Mr. Bature added. "Come and have breakfast and then we'll take you to your parents."

At that point, Samuel entered the room and switched on the radio. Before the horrified Batures could do anything, they heard the announcer repeat the news: "Among the schools burnt down was the Muslim High School at Station Road."

"Oh no, that's where my family lived!" Arike shrieked as she heard the news. Despite Mr. and Mrs. Bature's efforts to soothe her, she began to sob.

"Arike, don't cry," said Mr. Bature quickly. "I am sure your family is safe. I will go and bring them here. Samuel, you and Mary play with Arike while I drive down to find them."

"I'll go with you, Mr. Bature. I want to go with you," said Arike. However, Mr. and Mrs. Bature were able to convince Arike so stay behind while Mr. Bature went in search of her family.

An hour later, Mary heard the familiar sound of her father's car arriving. Looking out the window, she called to her friend, "Arike, come quickly. Your parents are here." As the girls ran out the door, Arike rushed into her parents' warm embrace.

"Safe, safe, praise be to Allah you are safe," said Arike's father as he lifted her playfully into the air.

"Yes, we are grateful to Allah . . . and also to the Batures," said Arike's mother. She gave Mary a hug.

Arike was anxious to know about her brothers and sisters. "How are Jide, Sade, Simi, and Bayo?" she asked.

"They are all waiting at government guest house, where we've been staying since the rioters burnt our house. You'll hear all about it when you get there."

Everyone was quiet for a while. Then Arike's father looked nervously at his watch. "We must go." Turning to the Batures, he said, "Thank you very much for your help. We are very grateful."

"Actually, it's Mary we should all thank. But for her, it wouldn't have ended like this."

Arike was too overcome to say anything to her friend. She hugged Mary and then went off with her parents.

Who Is the Cleverest?

William Russell Bascom, in his book *African Dilemma Tales* (1911), defines dilemma stories as "prose narratives that leave the listeners with a choice among alternatives." Such stories usually "involve discrimination on ethical, moral, or legal grounds." At the end of such a story, the listeners are usually asked to give their opinions and the reasons for them. This dilemma story is widely known throughout central Africa.

Three brothers once set out to wander. The first boy could hear very well. The second could count anything swiftly, no matter how numerous. The third could see farther and more clearly than anyone.

Now the three took a sack of millet with them, which they intended to use as their food. They had not gone very far when they came to a river. It was broad and wide, so they looked for a boat to go across, and soon found one. They loaded the millet into the boat, and then all three brothers carefully climbed in.

As they were crossing the river, the first brother said, "Oh, my! One of the kernels of millet has fallen into the water. I heard it."

The second brother said, "I will count the remaining kernels, to see if it is true." After he had completed his count, he said, "Yes, one kernel is missing."

The third brother said, "I will search for it." And he dove into the water. He saw it at the bottom of the river bed, picked it up, and swam back to the boat. "Here it is," he cried.

Tell me, which of the three boys was the cleverest?

How Anansi Spread Wisdom

Anansi (also spelled Ananse) is the trickster character found in many folk tales of Ghana and in the West African countries surrounding the territory that was once the Ashanti kingdom. Most stories in that part of the world are called Anansesem, whether they have the Anansi character or not, because it is believed all stories came from Anansi. Anansi is a spider but he is also a man. Most often, he is the one who tricks, but occasionally he is proven to be as foolish as any human. Here it is his baby son who teaches him a lesson. Many of these stories have short songs that are used in a call-and-response fashion. The music for the short, repetitive song given here appears in the companion volume to this one, *A World of Children's Songs.*

Anansi decided that he would sweep up all the knowledge and wisdom of the world and put it away in a safe place. Then, whenever a problem presented itself, he could take out as much wisdom as he needed to solve it. So Anansi went about carefully gathering wisdom and knowledge. When he found some he would put it into a gourd pot and then cover the pot tightly.

After Anansi had visited every corner of the kingdom, he was sure he had picked up all the wisdom and knowledge that was to be found. He had a big pot full of it, sealed shut. "Now I must find a safe place to put this pot," Anansi said to his wife.

He found a tall tree and decided he would hang up his pot of wisdom on the tallest branch. From some vines he made a strong string and tied it firmly all around the pot, leaving one end free. He wound the end of the string around his waist so that the pot hung down in front of him. Then, while his wife and baby son looked on, Anansi began to climb up the tree.

Kra, kra, kra, kra,
Climb, climb, climb, climb.
Mother, Mother! Tahinta! Tahinta! Tahinta!
Kra, kra, kra, kra,
Climb, climb, climb, climb.
Mother, Mother! Tahinta! Tahinta! Tahinta!

But no matter how he tried, he could not climb very well because the gourd pot full of wisdom kept getting in his way, bumping against his belly.

Anansi dropped down to the ground, and this time he tied the string around his neck. His wife and son watched him and wanted to say something, but Anansi would not let them speak. With the pot now held just under his chin, Anansi started to climb the tree again.

Kra, kra, kra, kra,
Climb, climb, climb, climb.
Mother, Mother! Tahinta! Tahinta! Tahinta!
Kra, kra, kra, kra,
Climb, climb, climb, climb.
Mother, Mother! Tahinta! Tahinta! Tahinta!

Anansi could not see where he was going because the pot forced his chin up so high. He tumbled down to the ground. He looked at the pot in disgust. His baby son, who was just learning to talk, said, "Daddy, carry it on your back."

Anansi tied the string around his shoulders in such a way that the pot hung down over his back. Once more he started up the tree.

Kra, kra, kra, kra,
Climb, climb, climb, climb.
Mother, Mother! Tahinta! Tahinta! Tahinta!

Kra, kra, kra, kra,
Climb, climb, climb, climb.
Mother, Mother! Tahinta! Tahinta! Tahinta!

This time Anansi managed to get to the very top of the tree with his pot of wisdom. When he looked down, he saw his little son smiling up at him. Anansi looked at his son and then at the pot of wisdom. He laughed aloud at himself. "I thought I had collected all the wisdom in the world, but even with all this knowledge, I could not figure out how to climb a tree while carrying a pot of wisdom. My son, who is so small, so small, so small—he has shown me that I did not gather all of it."

Anansi took the pot and threw it high up into the air. It landed on the ground and broke. Tseee! The wisdom scattered all over the kingdom. Anyone who wanted to could pick up some of it. And excuse my saying so, but you were a fool if you didn't go get some yourself.

That is my story. If it be sweet or if it be not sweet, take some of it elsewhere and let some come back to me.

Grasshopper and Toad
Retold by Amadou Dicko

The theme of this tale (pointing out the faults of others but overlooking one's own) can be found in many African folk tales. Here it is put in the very succinct form of the fable.

Grasshopper and Toad appeared to be good friends. People always saw them together. Yet they had never dined at each other's houses. One day Toad said to Grasshopper, "Dear friend, tomorrow come and dine at my house. My wife and I will prepare a special meal. We will eat it together."

The next day Grasshopper arrived at Toad's house. Before sitting down to eat, Toad washed his forelegs, and invited Grasshopper to do the same. Grasshopper did so, and it made a loud noise.

"Friend Grasshopper, can't you leave your chirping behind. I cannot eat with such a noise," said Toad.

Grasshopper tried to eat without rubbing his forelegs together, but it was impossible. Each time he gave a chirp, Toad complained and asked him to be quiet. Grasshopper was angry and could not eat. Finally, he said to Toad: "I invite you to my house for dinner, tomorrow."

The next day, Toad arrived at Grasshopper's home. As soon as the meal was ready, Grasshopper washed his forelegs, and invited Toad to do the same. Toad did so, and then hopped toward the food.

"You had better go back and wash again," said Grasshopper. "All that hopping in the dirt has made your forelegs dirty again."

Toad hopped back to the water jar, washed again, then hopped back to the table, and was ready to reach out for some food from one of the platters when Grasshopper stopped him: "Please don't put your dirty paws into the food. Go and wash them again."

Toad was furious. "You just don't want me to eat with you!" he cried. "You know very well that I must use my paws and forelegs in hopping about. I cannot help it if they get a bit dirty between the water jar and the table."

Grasshopper responded, "You are the one who started it yesterday. You know I cannot rub my forelegs together without making a noise."

From then on, they were no longer friends.

Moral: If you wish to have true friendship with someone, learn to accept each other's faults, as well as each other's good qualities.

Siime's Handkerchief
By Edreda Tuwangye

Many women and girls in East Africa wear a colorful cloth called a *kanga*. It is rectangular and large enough to wrap around the body. The *kanga* has beautiful designs and a Swahili saying on it. There is even a *kanga* that is meant to be a child's first picture book. The handkerchief in this story is like a miniature *kanga*, but it is unusual because it seems to have magical powers.

Siime saw a parcel on her bed. "A Christmas present for me?" she asked herself. She went to the bed and picked it up. There were words on it: "TO SIIME, WITH BEST WISHES." She opened the parcel. "A hanky! A beautiful hanky!" she shouted, jumping about.

Siime ran to her mother. She showed her the handkerchief.

"It's very beautiful!" her mother said.

Siime pointed to the pictures on the handkerchief. "Mama, look at the giraffe. It's got such a long neck. Look at the elephant. It's so fat but its tail is tiny. The zebra is wearing a beautiful dress. Eeee . . . and the small monkey! And the cock is ready to say 'Ko-ko-ko-ri-ko!' Mama, they are beautiful pictures. I love them. I love my hanky. Did you buy it for me?" Siime asked.

"No, Siime," said her mother.

"Mama, who did, then? You must know! Tell me Mama. Is it Tata? Is it Auntie Robina?"

"I don't know. But it's a very beautiful hanky. You are lucky to have it!" said her mother.

When Siime's father came, she ran to him. She showed him the handkerchief.

"It's a beautiful hanky. Who gave it to you?"

"Wasn't it you, Tata? I thought it was you. Mama said it wasn't her." "No, it wasn't me. It could be your Auntie Robina."

Auntie Robina came to visit. Siime ran to meet her. She showed her the pictures—the elephant, the zebra, the monkey, and the cock. "I love the animals. Don't you love them too? I like my hanky. Thank you for giving it to me, Auntie."

"It's a beautiful hanky. But I didn't give it to you," Auntie Robina said.

"It's got to be you! It isn't mother. It isn't father. Then who gave it to me? I found it on my bed. Someone must have put it there."

"Maybe a fairy did," said Auntie Robina.

For many days, Siime talked about her handkerchief. She told many stories about the animals in it. She showed the handkerchief to all her friends. They liked it and even wished it were theirs. They liked the giraffe, the elephant, the zebra, the monkey, and the cock. Akiiki was Siime's best friend. She too liked the hanky.

One day Siime lost her hanky. She looked everywhere for it. She looked in her school bag. She turned over her mattress. She looked under her bed. She put everything in her suitcase on the floor. Then she put each thing back one by one. The handkerchief was not there. She looked in the sitting room, in all the bedrooms, and in the kitchen. The handkerchief was not there. Siime's mother, father, and auntie helped her to look for the handkerchief, but they did not find it.

Akiiki came to play and Siime said to her, "Akiiki, I can't find my hanky. Did you pick it up and hide it? Do you want us to play hide-and-seek for it? We've looked everywhere and we can't find it. You'll give it to me, won't you? Akiiki, please do! I want my hanky back."

"But I don't have your hanky, Siime. I haven't seen it. I haven't touched it. I don't have your hanky. I did not hide it. You must have lost it." Akiiki looked scared.

"Then my hanky is lost," Siime cried.

Every night she prayed to have her handkerchief back.

One day Akiiki sat under a tree. She brought out the hanky. She had taken it from Siime's bag. She looked at the pictures and said, "How I wish these animals could talk. I could ask them many things."

As she said this, the animals came out of the handkerchief. They stood in front of her.

"Eee! Eee! Mama! Mama!" Akiiki cried with fear.

"Keep quiet!" all the animals shouted.

Tears ran down her face. She was shaking all over. She felt very bad.

The giraffe bent his long neck. He looked into Akiiki's face and said, "Akiiki, you told a lie. You took Siime's hanky, and you said you didn't take it."

The elephant lifted his trunk and said in a big voice, "Children must not tell lies."

"They must not take other people's hankies!" said the zebra, shaking his head.

The monkey pointed with his long arm and said, "Take it back. Take Siime's hanky back."

The cock beat his wings and shouted, "Ko-ko-ko-riko! Go! Go! Go! Ko-ko-ko-riko! Now! Now! Now!"

All the animals made a ring around Akiiki and sang:

"Take it back.
Go! Go! Go!
Take it back.
Now! Now! Now!"

Akiiki cried more and more. She was very unhappy. She said, "I am sorry. I'll take Siime's hanky back. I will never steal again. And I'll never tell lies again."

Then all the animals went back into the handkerchief. Akiiki folded the handkerchief. She made a nice parcel. She wrote on it: "TO SIIME. I AM SORRY. FROM AKIIKI, YOUR BEST FRIEND." She took the parcel to Siime.

Siime opened it. And what did she see? The handkerchief. She jumped for joy and sang:

My beautiful hanky is back!
Giraffe is back!
Zebra is back!
Monkey is back!
Cock is back!
And the fat elephant is also back.

Then, hand in hand, Siime and Akiiki went out to play.

The Husband and Wife Who Wanted to Have a Child

The handkerchief has been in common use for only about 300 years. Prior to that, the handkerchief was carried mostly by people in the theater or at court. When ordinary persons began to realize it was socially and hygienically more acceptable to use a handkerchief, rather than one's fingers or the edge of a sleeve or hem of a skirt, they began to train their children always to have a handkerchief handy. Out of this teaching came a number of figures and short little stories that use a handkerchief—usually the large, white type now used almost exclusively by men. Here is a story combining two of the most commonly known figures. You will need three handkerchiefs to tell it. Before starting the story, make two dolls using two handkerchiefs according to the following instructions:

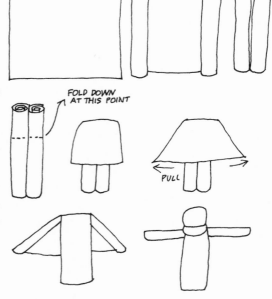

Lay a handkerchief flat.

Roll each side to the middle. When finished, each "roll" should be about an inch in diameter.

Fold down about two-fifths of the rolls.

Separate the folded-down rolls, pulling apart the rolls but not entirely undoing them.

Carefully turn the entire figure over and tie up the two pulled-apart ends, so that they make arms. This is Mr. Hanky Panky.

Repeat the process with a second handkerchief.

Then, once the arms are tied in place, turn the figure over again and spread the lower rolls out, so as to suggest a skirt. That will be Mrs. Hanky Panky.

Lay them side by side, and next to them lay out the third handkerchief, folded in half as a triangle, with the point up.

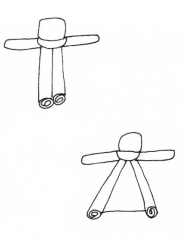

There was once a husband and wife, Mr. and Mrs. Hanky Panky, who wanted more than anything else to have a child. They waited and waited, but no child came. At last, when they had almost given up hope, the wife discovered she was going to have a child. She and her husband were so happy. They began to prepare many things for their baby. They made a cradle.

Begin rolling the two side points inward.

Continue rolling while saying the following:

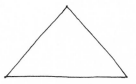

They sewed a set of tiny clothes for the baby.

They made some special toys and playthings.

They made everything ready.

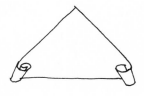

Complete the two rolls. Turn figure over, being careful not to let it unroll.

But what a surprise!

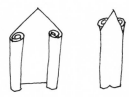

Take hold of top upper corner and pull down gently until it covers bottom part of figure.

For when the baby arrived it was not one baby—it was TWINS!

Flip entire figure over gently.

And here they are in their cradle.

Hold at the two tips and rock back and forth, as though rocking a cradle. The twins are the two rolls inside.

The Little White Rabbit
Translated by Henriquetta Monteiro

This cumulative folk tale follows many of the patterns typical of such tales in Europe. The requests go to the largest animal first and then on down to smaller and less powerful creatures. It is usually the tiniest one who achieves success. The rhyme was probably sung in olden days.

Once a little white rabbit went off to a garden to get something to eat for dinner. When she returned to her home, she heard a noise from within, which frightened her a bit. So she sang out:

"I'm the little white rabbit
Come home from the garden
Where I pulled up a cabbage
To make me some soup."

In answer, the rabbit heard a great gruff voice from within:

"I'm the huge horned goat;
With a spring and a bound
I can cut you in three,
And eat you up in no time."

The poor little rabbit ran away in fright. She ran until she met up with a big bull. She said to him: "Big Bull, my friend,
I'm the white rabbit
That went to the garden
And brought home a cabbage
To make me some soup.
When I got there I found
The huge horned goat;

With a spring and a bound
He will cut me in three
And eat me up in no time."

The bull replied: "I can't help you. I won't go near that huge horned goat."

The rabbit went on farther until she met a big dog. She cried out to him in a pleading voice: "Dear Dog, do help me.

I'm the white rabbit
That went into the garden
And brought home a cabbage
To make me some soup.
When I got there I found
A huge horned goat.
With a spring and a bound
He will cut me in three
And eat me up in no time."

The dog replied very politely: "Oh, I can't go there. It would be much too dangerous for me."

The rabbit set off again until she saw a rooster strutting about. She called to the rooster in her most tearful voice: "Oh please, good Rooster,

I'm the white rabbit
That went into the garden
And brought home a cabbage
To make me some soup.
When I got there I found
The huge horned goat.
With a spring and a bound
He will cut me in three
And eat me up in no time."

But the rooster just stalked off, saying "I don't go near such ferocious beasts."

The poor little rabbit was in despair. Her home had been taken over and no one would help her get it back. Suddenly she came upon a busy ant, carrying a load twice the ant's size. The ant looked at her and asked kindly:

"What is the matter, Rabbit? Why do you look so sad?"

"I'm the little white rabbit
That went to the garden
And brought home a cabbage
To make me some soup.
When I got there I found
The huge horned goat.
With a spring and a bound
He will cut me in three
And eat me up in no time."

When the ant heard the rabbit's tale, she said, "I will go with you and see what we can do."

They returned to the rabbit's house together and knocked at the door. The great, gruff voice answered from within:

"Here no one can enter
For I am the huge horned goat.
With a spring and a bound
I can cut you in three
And eat you up in no time."

The rabbit was too frightened to answer, but the little ant said,

"I'm the great big ant
That can make a hole in your belly
So big it will turn your insides to jelly."

As soon as the ant said these words, she quietly crept through the keyhole. Then she crawled across the floor, climbed up to the goat's belly, and gave it a big sting. The goat thought it was a giant ant about to make a hole in his belly that would turn his insides to jelly. He dashed out the door and ran for the hillside, forgetting all about the rabbit.

And the little ant—did she go with him? No, she jumped off and stayed with her friend the rabbit. And they lived together very happily ever after.

The Story of the Water Lily
By Grozdana Olujic
Translated by Jascha Kessler

Grozdana Olujic lives in Belgrade and writes in Serbo-Croatian. Just as Hans Christian Andersen did a century ago, she likes to compose stories in the fairy tale mode, with an unusual twist at the end.

The river and the mountain once fell to quarreling, so the river changed its course. But it also left one of its sources behind, a captive in the valley.

Naturally, the mountain laughed, boasting, "You're no river now. You're my prisoner!" And the stream shrank and grew sad. Little by little it became a marsh, where reeds sprouted. The fish folk all retreated before a mob of invading frogs. The mountain mocked, "What a dismal sight you are! You have no fish, and you have no flowers—you're worthless!"

The marsh bent her head in shame. The mobs of frogs grew to a multitude. They were frogs of every kind: big, small, gray, green, and spotted ones.

"What pretty ones my children are!" croaked the bullfrog proudly. Then she drew back. For pity's sake, what's this?" the bullfrog said, dismayed, staring at a tadpole. Its voice was loud, and its eyes were clear, although it still wore its stump of a tail. No matter—that would soon dwindle away. But just look at its color! Never before had any frog been born all white. Where had this creature come from? Whose child could this be?

The bullfrog told everybody, asking the frog folk to find this white frog's parents. In vain. None of them would admit that she was their daughter.

Rejected by everyone and miserable because of her color, the white frog began to spend lonely days gazing at her reflection. Soon she stopped sleeping and singing. Until one morning she heard a long sigh.

The white frog turned her head left and right—there was nobody to be seen. She tried hard to find who it could be. Look! It was the marsh that sighed so heavily, so deeply. Out of the muddy bottom a bubble climbed, imploring the sun in a delicate voice to dry her up, to turn her into a cloud or nothing at all. "I'm ugly, and nobody wants me. I have no fish and no flowers. What good is life to me?"

It seemed to the white frog that it was also her own unhappiness the marsh was lamenting. For she was ugly and despised by all. Still, she loved the rays of the sun, and she loved the wind. The murmuring reeds and the dancing butterflies enchanted her.

The white frog grew thoughtful: if the marsh disappeared, all the frogs and reeds would perish; the birds and butterflies would all fly away. Why had she not thought of it before? Butterflies! One of them might be the flower of the marsh. The white frog begged the gaudy beauties to stop for a moment, but none of them wanted to be a marsh flower.

The white frog sighed. She asked the stars to help her. At last she called to the brightest star. But that one replied harshly, "Stop talking nonsense, white frog! What star would ever consent to come down to be a mere marsh flower? Find some other fool!"

The white frog retreated. Distraught with sorrow, she addressed the rising sun. "Before you change into a golden rose, O King of Heaven, please won't you stop for a while and be the flower of the marsh?"

The sun regarded the white frog with curiosity and smiled. "I am in a hurry. But there's no need for me to stop." And with his golden finger, the King of Heaven touched the white frog.

"Don't you see that you are the flower of the marsh? A lily!" With the touch of the sun's finger, the white frog felt herself changing.

Awed, the frog folk plunged to the bottom of the marsh and burrowed deep in the mud.

Who knows how long they hid down there?

When they swam back up to the surface again, the white frog was gone. But a great white flower was shining gloriously in the very place where she had lived her lonely days.

It happened a long time ago, when the world was made. And to this day the marsh and the waterlily are always together.

The Bear and the Three Granddaughters
Translated and adapted by Anne Pellowski

The bear is found in many Russian and Polish folktales. Sometimes he is clever and outwits humans, but many times, quick thinking on the part of certain individuals allows them to get the better of bears. In this case it is three girls, who have learned their lessons well.

There were once three girls who were often naughty. One day their parents said, "We shall send you to live with your grandmother. She is very wise. Perhaps she can do something with you."

And truth to tell, Granny did know how to handle those girls. She taught them many things, but she always gave them plenty of time to play together, after they had done their work.

One fine day the girls wanted to go out and play in the meadow near the forest.

"Granny, please, may we go?" they begged politely. "We promise to bring you a basketful of mushrooms."

"Very well, run along then," said Granny. "But don't go too far into the forest."

The girls sped off to the meadow. They played for a while and then began to search for mushrooms. But they did not find many.

"Let's go into the forest," said the oldest. "The best and biggest mushrooms can always be found under trees. We won't go far."

They moved from tree to tree. Soon they had picked a big basketful of mushrooms. But the girls were now far into the dense forest. Suddenly, from the thickets came a crashing and crackling. Out stepped a big bear.

"Hmmm, Hmmm," grunted the bear. "You will make a fine set of servants for me." He grabbed the girls and dragged them off to his big underground home, hidden in the middle of the dark forest.

"You—keep the place clean," growled the bear to the oldest girl. To the middle girl he grunted: "You mind the fire." And to the youngest: "You cook the food."

The girls wept and cried but there was nothing to be done. For a few days they worked for the bear, all the while thinking of some way to escape. At last, the youngest girl had an idea.

She went to the bear and pleaded with him: "Bear, let me go home for just one day. I want to take Granny a gift, to show her that we are still alive. If she does not hear from us soon, she will come searching, with the hunter."

"Certainly not," growled the bear. "If I let you go, you would run away and never come back. I myself will take your gift to your grandmother. But what do you intend to send so that she will know it comes from you?"

"Granny taught us to make delicious plum dumplings. We will make a big dish of dumplings," said all three girls.

"Hmmm, hmmm, very well," grunted the bear.

The girls built up the fire, boiled the water, and made a big batch of plum dumplings. When they were ready, the youngest girl piled them into a deep dish and then went to get a large basket. Then she called out to the bear: "Bear, the dumplings are ready. I shall place them carefully in this big basket. You can carry it on your back. But you must promise not to open the basket or touch the dumplings. Before you leave, I intend to climb a tall tree so that I can keep my eye on you."

"Hmmm, hmmm, all right," groaned the bear. He was about to put the basket on his back, when the youngest girl interrupted him.

"Go outside and see if the weather is fine. We cannot have the dumplings get wet. Granny would not recognize them as ours," said the little girl.

As soon as the bear left the underground home, the three girls jumped into each other's arms and climbed into the basket. The youngest pulled the big dish of dumplings over her head. Then they waited.

The bear returned, saw that the basket was ready, and lifted it up to his shoulders. He set off for Grandmother's house, at the edge of the village. He lumbered along through the trees but soon he got tired. When he came to a large tree stump, he stopped.

"Hmmm, hmmm. I think I shall have a dumpling," he grunted.

But before he could take the basket off his back and open it, he heard a little girl's voice say: "Don't touch the dumplings!" The voice seemed to come from a tree overhead.

"That girl certainly has sharp eyes," thought the bear. He continued on his way through the forest. After a time, he came to another tree stump. He was ready to take a short rest and eat a dumpling.

But once more a voice called out from above, a bit fainter: "Don't sit down and don't touch the dumplings!"

On and on went the bear through groves of trees until he finally arrived at the meadow at the edge of the forest. There was another tree stump.

"I need a rest," grumbled the bear. "And I shall have a dumpling, too. Surely that girl cannot see me now."

But from above came a soft voice, as from a distance: "I see you! Don't touch the dumplings."

"Fancy that! I've come all this way and still she can see me!" cried the bear as he hurried across the meadow. He arrived at Granny's house and knocked loudly at the gate.

"Open up," growled the bear, "I've brought you a gift from

your granddaughters."

But he made so much noise that all the dogs of the village heard him and came running, barking in unison. They startled him so much that he dropped the basket by the gate and lumbered back into the forest.

When Granny came to the gate, there was the basket, standing all by itself. She lifted the lid, and out popped the three girls. They danced for joy and Granny agreed that they were clever girls to have tricked the bear in that way.

"And what delicious plum dumplings you have made," she said as soon as she had tasted them. "I think you are now ready to go back to your parents."

And as soon as they had eaten all the plum dumplings—they did!

Enough Bread
Translated and adapted by Anne Pellowski

This story rhyme is adapted from a Polish nursery rhyme. I like to recite it, using a set of six or more nesting dolls to symbolize the mother, the aunt, the grandmother, and the children.

A hungry brood
    looked for food;
But the shelf was bare.
Mother came,
    saw the same;
Called her children and spoke to them:
"Who will get some bread?"
Off went one,
    bought a bun;
Came back home, on the run.
She put the bun on the pantry shelf.
Next day it was gone.
Auntie came,
    searched in vain;
Turned to the children and said again:
"Once more
    go to the store;
Buy a *loaf* of bread."
One more
    went to the store;
Bought a loaf of bread.
She put the loaf in a wooden box.
Next day it was gone.

Granny came
    looked in vain;
Turned to the children and said again:
"Once more
    go to the store;
Buy a bag of flour."
One more
    went to the store.
Bought a bag of flour
She put the bag in Granny's arms.
Next day—there was bread!

The Bad Child
By Eveline Hasler

Sometimes, writers exaggerate the good or bad aspects of their characters so as to make a point. Who is really "bad" in this story? Think of proverbs and sayings such as: "Like father, like son," "A tree is known by its fruit," or "As the twig is bent, so inclines the tree."

When the child was a baby, it lay in the stroller and clenched its hands into tiny red fists.

The mother said to herself, "I'm glad it's a girl. Girls are less wild than boys. They don't make as much mess. They are more obedient." Dreamily, she stared at her old childhood doll resting in its ruffly dress among the pillows on the sofa. It had a sweet face with rounded lips and soft, plump hands with tiny lacquered fingernails. "Later," thought the mother, "my little girl will look just like that. People will stop and stare when we go for a Sunday walk in the park."

Time passed. As the little girl grew and learned to walk and talk, her mother had a hard time with her. The girl often grabbed the tablecloth and pulled it off the table, dishes and all. She paged through books and tore the pages. When she was supposed to eat her vegetable purée, she closed her mouth tight and instead smeared the purée on the table. Once she hit her mother's hand with her spoon. Her mother hit her back. The girl cried. The mother stared at her, taking in the dirty overalls, the angry face, the runny nose.

"I imagined a little girl would be something quite different," she thought. "I wanted a sweet, dear little thing, someone I could love and take on walks. Instead, I have someone who dirties the apartment and prevents me from doing my housework."

Every morning the mother put her child out in the garden so that she could clean the house properly. In front of the house was a small area laid out with bumpy stones. In front of that, all along a dirty slatted fence, was a vegetable patch with all sorts of green things. In the corner, where it was shady most of the time, stood a pine tree with a mossy base. The branches of the pine tree looked like the dark wings of birds of prey.

The child dug around in the sandbox. She had no brothers or sisters and there were no children living next door. Year after year she grew more bored. In winter she threw snowballs, in summer, stones at the birds or at cats.

"She is a very wild child," said the mother to the vegetable seller. "Luckily, she will soon go to school."

The little girl was now six years old and looking forward to school. She was happy that at last she would get away from the house, the tiny yard with the pine tree, the slatted wood fence, and the sandbox.

The school stood at the end of the street. The girl stood at the fence and peered at the children as they passed on their way to school.

"Good morning!" she called out. But they just went on by without reacting.

"They could at least look in this direction and say a few words," she thought. Under the pine tree was a small area of leftover snow. She gathered some of it up into a hard ball and threw it over the fence at a group of passing children. One of the boys stopped, felt around his neck, and brought out small lumps of snow from under his collar. He glanced in the direction from which the snowball had come. Between two slats of wood he saw a small, frosty-red face.

"G' morning," said the girl expectantly.

"Snotnose!" jeered the boy. He lifted a piece of ice from the edge of the street and swung it threateningly in his hand.

The girl pulled back from the fence, shocked. She threw no more stones or snowballs. One morning a woman walked past the fence, leading a dachshund on a leash.

"Hi, doggy," said the little girl. The dog paid her no attention. It had short, nimble legs under its barrel-shaped body and smooth, reddish brown hair. "Stay here a while, you nice dog; look at me!" The girl threw a snowball to get the dog's attention. It barely touched the dog, but the woman came back a few steps. Her face appeared above the slatted fence. It was narrow and pale, with sharp, thin lips.

"What's your name?" she asked.

The girl gave her name.

"Do you go to school?"

"I start in April."

"So. So," said the woman. "I had better note down your name." She pulled on the leash and left without saying goodbye. The girl listened to the staccato sound of her steps. She stood on the base of the fence and saw the woman enter the schoolhouse at the end of the street.

The rest of the snow melted. On the tips of tree branches appeared light green buds. It was April.

The girl hopped as she skipped along to school, held by her mother's hand. The walls of the school shone through the still bare limbs of the chestnut trees. Doves fluttered around the cornices and window ledges.

For the girl the school was a castle full of secrets.

Once inside, a woman typed out the name, address, and birth date of the new student. As soon as the mother gave the girl's name, the woman looked up from her typing and stared at the girl.

"So, here she is then!" Her fingers stopped typing. "A real wild one, isn't she?" Through her sharply reflecting eyeglasses the woman glanced questioningly at the mother.

"Yes, it's a good thing she's starting school," said the mother. She sighed.

The woman stood up, came out from behind her type-writer, and led the child to a classroom where there were already quite a few seats filled. She passed the girl on to the teacher with a whisper: "A special case. You'd do well to keep your eye on her. Not long ago she threw a snowball at my dachshund."

The teacher placed the child in the front row. The girl was allowed to unpack her notebooks and colored pencils. Then she was supposed to make lines on a piece of paper. Her hand, which until then had only dug in the sand or played around with a snow shovel, grasped hard around a red pencil and started to draw the line. The teacher stood behind her desk, watching her. The teacher's glance seemed like a weight on the girl's arm. Her palm sweated and her fingers got cramped. With the whole weight of her upper body, she pushed the pencil across the paper, and slit it as though she had cut it with a knife.

The girl got frightened. With her left hand she covered the place where she had slit the paper and tried again to make the correct lines.

"What are you hiding?" asked the teacher. Suddenly, she was standing right behind the girl's desk.

"Nothing," stammered the girl.

But the teacher lifted the girl's arm away from the paper.

"Aha!" she cried. "You mess up your paper and then lie about it. And on your first day of school."

At recess the new students stood around in a thick bunch in the schoolyard, like sheep. They bit into their sandwiches or apples. Those who were now in second grade walked by with knowing expressions. Suddenly one of them, a boy, stopped and yelled out: "There she is, that booby bug; always standing by the fence. Now you'll get it back for your snowball."

He ran to the girl, caught hold of her collar, and shook her so hard she could hardly see or hear anything. Her classmates only stared at her.

At noon many of the new pupils were picked up by their mothers.

"Just think, we have a bad child in our class," said one of the girls to her mother.

"Well, just so you don't play with her," said the mother.

So, from the first day on, the girl was known as "the bad child," and the other children didn't even stop to think that she could have an ordinary name, like Margaret.

The little girl tried hard not to be a bad child. But often, out of fear of being a bad child, she did stupid things.

The next day, a boy who wanted to take his notebook up to show the teacher stumbled over her foot that was stretched out in the aisle. She had only stretched it out because it was more comfortable sitting that way, rather than cramped under the desk. But the boy shouted angrily, "You did that on purpose." She wanted to say something, but she saw right away it was no use. The boy stuck his tongue out at her.

Later she accidentally spilled paint on the notebook of the girl who sat in the desk next to her. The next day, that girl brought a note from her mother, asking the teacher to allow her daughter to sit in another seat. So she was given a desk in a corner, all by herself.

"Do they think I'm some kind of dangerous animal?" the girl asked herself. At recess, no one spoke to her. Sometimes, classmates would walk behind her and secretly give her a push. At that the bad child became wild with anger and struck out with her fists or scratched with her nails. The other children would laugh and scream, "Bite and scratch, wildcat."

Once, after she had become especially angry at something they did to her in recess, she ran back to the classroom to wash her face in the sink there. In the mirror above the sink she saw her red-flecked cheeks, her messed-up hair, and her darkly glowing eyes. They gleamed just like those of a wildcat. She got frightened.

She would have liked nothing better than to have a sweet face with a lovely mouth, just like the sofa doll in her house.

"But I look like a bad child, so I must be one," she said to herself. From then on, she gave up trying to be good. "It can't be helped," she thought. "So I'll just show them how bad I can be. Horribly bad."

Every day she got worse. She stuck pins in her classmates and messed up their notebooks. Once, she even took a scissors and cut a jacket hanging in the cloakroom.

One morning the teacher stood sternly behind her desk and said: "Children, this morning I left a black change purse in my coat pocket. I now find that the purse is gone. One of you must have stolen it."

"I didn't," shouted a child immediately. "I didn't either," "Not me," the class murmered as one. Suddenly all was quiet. They turned their heads in the direction of the bad child. She said nothing.

"Did you come into the classroom at recess?" asked the teacher.

"No," said the bad child.

As soon as school was out that day, the children surrounded the girl and shouted at her, all together, "Scratcher and biter, liar and stealer."

The bad child tried to get by but a boy grabbed her by the arm and held her fast. At that she turned her head around and bit his hand.

"Ow!" he shrieked and pulled his bleeding hand away.

The girl sprang away, jumped over the hawthorn hedge, and ran into the street. The other children ran after her. When they saw they could not catch up with her, they started throwing stones at her. It was a mean and dangerous thing to do, but because they were throwing them at a bad child, they thought they were doing a good thing.

One big stone hit the bad child. With her hand she felt behind her head, wobbled a bit, and then fell down. Her collar was now red with blood.

"She's dead," cried one of the children, horrified. But none of them dared to go near the fallen girl. As soon as they saw a car enter the street and put on its brakes, one of the children cried out, "Let's run. The police are coming."

Later, they peeked through the hawthorn hedge surrounding the school and watched as the ambulance came. Two men in white picked up the bad child, put her on a stretcher, and took her away.

But the bad child was not dead. As she finally came to, and opened her eyes a bit, she saw so much white surrounding her that she closed her eyes again, tight. Toward evening, she opened them again, and it appeared as though a new layer of snow lay over her room. Shadows danced over it, like the moving pictures in a film. She saw herself once again running into the street, pursued by the others. She felt again the heavy weight of the stone as it hit her head.

"My head," she thought, and with her hand touched her forehead; but all she felt was a bandage that barely left her eyes, nose, and mouth uncovered.

She felt frightened and began to cry. Out of the whiteness came a nurse. She bent over the little girl with a smile, and gave her a drink out of a sipper cup.

"You must lie still, Margaret," said the nurse. "Soon you will feel better."

After a while the girl noticed that she was not alone in the room. There were other beds, and in each bed lay a child.

On the fifth day, she was able to lift her head from the pillow a bit.

"Oh, Margaret is awake," whispered a girl with a long

braid who lay in the bed next to hers. She was talking to another girl who sat, all dressed up, on a bed across the room.

Six pairs of eyes settled expectantly on the new girl, as though they had all been waiting only for the moment when the new patient would wake up and talk to them.

"Good morning, Margaret. You slept such a long time," said the girl with the long braid.

"We all had to be very still; we couldn't run around or laugh too loud," said the girl who was dressed. She had a doll in front of her and was combing its hair.

"Look, Margaret, I have a head bandage just like you," said a third girl, who lay in the bed by the wall.

"Do you have a hole in your head like I do?" asked Margaret weakly.

"No," she laughed. "Only something with my ears that had to be corrected."

The children laughed often now, and sometimes the nurse came in and said, "Lisbeth! Ria! Monica! Margaret!" and put her finger to her lips to show they were making too much noise. Sometimes, when the new girl lay very still on her back, she thought she was a feather, floating around in the room. She lay there in happiness, filled at the wonder of hearing herself called—Margaret.

Days went by. The girl with the corrected ears went home and another took her place. Margaret was allowed to dress and get out of bed. She felt better and stronger every day. When the nurse came in with meal trays, Margaret could help pour out the tea. Sometimes she helped the nurse carry away the trays of dirty dishes or make the beds.

After four weeks, Margaret was allowed to go home.

"Too bad that you have to go," said the other children. "We had so much fun together. Give us your address. Let's write each other."

"And I'll visit you," promised Margaret.

"We will miss you," said the nurse. "You were so patient, even when your head hurt so much. And later, you helped us a lot. You were really a dear, Margaret."

On the day after the next, Margaret returned to school. As soon as she entered the yard, the children broke off playing and whispered to one another, "Look, the bad child is here again."

Margaret did not jump at them, scratching and biting. While the other children stared, she went right by them, climbed the steps, and went to her classroom.

The room was empty. She went to the sink and looked in the mirror above it. She looked hard at her face. There were no wildcat eyes there any more.

"Hi, Margaret," she said to herself, nodding and laughing. Then she went to her seat, took out her notebooks, and waited for the lessons to start.

America
North of the Rio Grande

How Medicine Came to the People

The Ojibway are a group of Native American peoples of the Algonquian language group. Their culture is similar to that of most Eastern Woodland groups, but it has its own distinctive patterns as well. At one time they were the largest group of tribes living north of Mexico. They controlled the entire Great Lakes area and parts of what later became the states of North Dakota and Iowa. One of the main characters in stories of the Ojibway is Manabozho, also called Nanabush or Weesakejak. He is sometimes a trickster, sometimes a messenger, sometimes a deeply spiritual leader. At times he takes human form and at other times he is an animal, usually the Great Hare.

In the early years, the first humans were living on the island home that had been created for them on the back of a great turtle. For a long time, things went well there. But then a disease came, spreading sickness among them. Many people died. Among those who died was a young boy. The Great Spirit took pity on the child and called for Manabozho.

"Manabozho," said the Great Spirit, "take this boy back to the land of the living, and give the people there the medicine they need to live." The Great Spirit then handed Manabozho and the boy a bundle in which was tied up the wisdom and healing that humans needed in order to live healthy lives.

Manabozho set out with the young child. They went into a deep forest and at nightfall lay down to sleep. Manabozho had a dream. In the dream he saw an otter carrying a branch in its mouth. When Manabozho awoke, he knew he must search for an otter who would help him take healing to the people. Manabozho and the boy traveled for a long time; the boy was almost a young man when they came to a great lake. There, swimming playfully along the banks, they saw an otter. They called to the otter, but at first it paid no attention to them. They called and called, making noises such as an otter makes. At last, they got the otter to notice them. "You must come along with us, Otter," said Manabozho. "It is up to us to bring the healing ways to the people." And Manabozho convinced the otter to come along with them.

The three traveled on their long journey. They had many adventures and had to stop many times. The youth became a mature man. At last they came to a vast body of water and in it was the island home of the humans. Manabozho, the man, and the otter could see that the people looked sickly and weak. Many appeared to to be starving and were wandering aimlessly around.

"They do not have the power of the four directions," said Otter. Otter dove into the water and swam close to the island, calling out to the people, "Look carefully at what I am doing." Otter swam to the east and then back to the center of the lake. Otter swam to the south and then back to the center. Otter swam to the west and then back to the center. Otter swam to the north and then back to the center. Otter showed the people how to always find the center, and how to be aware of the four directions, so that they could always be in harmony with the space they lived in.

Then Otter swam away and returned to its original home. Manabozho took the man back to his people, and they rejoiced to see him back among the living. Manabozho and the man took out the healing plants they had brought with them and began to make medicines to help the sick. They also showed the people how to find the balance between their bodies and their souls, so that they would fall sick less often. They shared the wise advice that was in the bundle sent by the Great Spirit:

Cherish wisdom.	Live peacefully.
Respect all life.	Honor your promises.
Be courageous.	Be honest.
Live moderately.	Share your gifts.

And for a long time after that the people lived in harmony with one another and with all that surrounded them.

Ti-Jean and the White Cat

In folktales, Ti-Jean, short for Petit Jean, is the French Canadian equivalent of the English Jack and the Spanish Juan. He often plays the role of wise fool, but in this story he appears as the lucky youngest son.

There was once a king who had three sons—one called Cordon-bleu, one called Cordon-vert, and the youngest, Ti-Jean. One day the king said, "You are now all grown up. The one of you who can find me the most beautiful horse will have my crown."

The three young men set off down the road. They came to a place where three roads branched off. "I'll take this road," said Cordon-bleu. "And I'll take this one," said Cordon-vert. So Ti-Jean had to take the one that was left. The three brothers agreed on a day and time to meet again at the same spot.

Ti-Jean walked and walked until he came to the end of the road. He saw a path leading into a forest, so he took that. Before long he came upon a little straw house. In front of it he saw a white cat and four toads. They were carrying water to a big vat. When they had filled the vat with water, the white cat threw in the four toads, and with a "Miao, miao!" jumped in after them. In a moment, out of the water stepped a dripping wet girl.

"What do you want?" she asked Ti-Jean.

"A horse," replied Ti-Jean. We are three sons, and my father, the king, has promised his crown to the one who can bring back the best horse."

"Tomorrow I will once again be the white cat. You must go into my stable and select the largest and mangiest of my toads.

Ride it back to your father, and you will see that the next day it will be transformed into the handsomest horse on earth."

The next morning, Ti-Jean mounted the toad and set off down the road, *patati, patata*, as though he were riding a horse. When he came to the spot where the three roads branched off, there were his two brothers waiting for him. Each of them had a prancing horse. They saw Ti-Jean on his toad and said, "Better not show that to our father, he will laugh you out of the country." But Ti-Jean just set off behind his brothers, *patati, patata*, urging his toad on with gentle taps.

They arrived home late and put the two horses and the toad in the stable. The next morning Cordon-bleu and Cordon-vert got up early and went off to show their horses to their father. "And what about Ti-Jean?" asked the king. "Oh, he has only a toad," they laughed.

Ti-Jean got up later and went to the stable. There, in the stall where he had left his toad, was the handsomest horse he had ever seen, with a silvery mane tipped in gold.

"Oh!" cried the king when he saw the horse. "Ti-Jean has brought the best horse. He has won. But you know that a king has the right to three demands. So you must set off again and the one who brings me the most finely woven cloth will have my crown."

The three set off again, and once more they took the same roads. Ti-Jean followed the path into the woods and came upon the little straw house. There was the white cat, carrying water with her three toads. Ti-Jean sat down and looked at her. As soon as the vat was full, with a "Miao, Miao!" the cat threw the toads into the water and jumped in after them. In a moment, out stepped the girl. This time she looked less bedraggled.

"Ti-Jean, what are you looking for?" she asked.

"I am looking for a piece of cloth of the finest weave," said Ti-Jean.

"Tomorrow morning I shall once again be changed into

the white cat. Look in my chest of drawers; there you will find an ordinary walnut. Put it in your pocket and take it home with you. Ask your father to break open the walnut and out will come 30 ells of the finest cloth ever woven."

Cordon-bleu and Cordon-vert met at the branching of the three roads. They each carried pieces of cloth. But when Ti-Jean arrived, carrying the walnut in his pocket, they could see no sign of any cloth.

"Haven't you found any?" they asked him. Ti-Jean said only, "I think that with all the cloth you have there, Father will have enough."

The next morning they appeared before the king to show the cloth they had brought. That which Cordon-bleu had brought was soft and shimmery. "I think Ti-Jean could not find any," he said. But Ti-Jean placed the walnut on a table in front of his father and told him to break it open.

When the king saw the gorgeous cloth that erupted from the walnut he said, "Ti-Jean has won again. But as I said before, a king can make three demands, so here is the last one. The one who brings back the cleverest, loveliest girl will have my crown."

The three sons set off again, and again they took the same roads. Ti-Jean followed the same path to the little straw house in the middle of the woods. Sure enough, there was the white cat, carting water with her toads. When the vat was full, with a "Miao, miao!" she jumped in. In a moment, the same girl appeared, but this time she seemed like a princess to Ti-Jean.

"Ti-Jean, this is the third time you have come. Why are you here this time?" asked the girl.

"My father, the king, had three commands. For the last one he said to us: 'Whichever son brings back the cleverest, loveliest girl shall have my crown.' I have not met anyone cleverer or lovelier than you, so I would like you to come back with me."

"I have been put under a spell," said the girl, and it can be broken only if the son of a king agrees to marry me."

"That's fine with me," agreed Ti-Jean. "We will marry as soon as we return to my father."

"Tomorrow I will once again be the white cat," the girl reminded him. "You must be willing to take me to your father in that form. Harness my three toads to the old carriage in the stable, and we can ride together."

The next morning Ti-Jean did as he was told. When the brothers arrived at the crossroads, Ti-Jean saw that they were accompanied by two pretty girls. When the older brothers saw Ti-Jean in the old-fashioned carriage pulled by big, fat toads, they looked in vain for a girl. Seated next to Ti-Jean was a white cat. They saw how she purred contentedly and sat up smartly at Ti-Jean's arm.

"Is that all you have to show for your search?" laughed the brothers.

The next morning, Cordon-bleu and Cordon-vert appeared before the king with their chosen brides. "And what about Ti-Jean?" asked the king. "He has brought only a pet white cat," answered the brothers. "I want to see her," said the king.

In that moment, Ti-Jean entered with his bride at his side. She was the cleverest, loveliest creature anyone had ever seen. Behind them were four splendid horses and a coach the like of which even the king did not own.

"It is Ti-Jean who has won my crown," said the king, and he lifted it off his head and put it on Ti-Jean.

Well, what a celebration they had for the weddings. I was there. But I haven't been back since then so I don't know what is happening there now.

Brer Rabbit and the Rock Soup

There are variants of this story told around the world. In most of them, the trick succeeds. There is disagreement as to whether Brer Rabbit was a folktale character brought by blacks from Africa or whether the character was picked up from Native Americans or other groups living in America or was a combination of several sources. Whichever it was, Brer Rabbit became a central character of many African American folktales.

One way Brer Rabbit made his living was like this. In his pocket he carried a smooth, pretty rock, about the size of a turkey egg. Then he would go off to people who were not acquainted with his tricks and he would pass himself off as a first-class cook. He would say, "I have a rock here and with it I can make the best-tasting soup you ever ate."

He went to Brer Bear's house and said just that, so Brer Bear asked him to make some rock soup. Brer Rabbit put the pot on the fire, boiled some water, and then dropped in the stone.

"It tastes even better with some meat and vegetables thrown in," said Brer Rabbit. So Brer Bear brought first a bit of meat and then some vegetables.

"You probably like your own seasoning," said Brer Rabbit. And Brer Bear admitted he did and brought his own seasoning, which Brer Rabbit added to the pot. Then he stirred the soup and let it simmer and let it simmer more and stirred it again.

It did make a nice soup. It fooled Brer Bear. He thought it was the rock that gave the rich flavor to the soup. Brer Rabbit got a big dinner at Brer Bear's house that day.

Another time when Brer Rabbit was very hungry he went to Brer Raccoon's house and fooled him in the same way. Brer Rabbit did this for some time, going from house to house.

One day he went to Brer Fox's house and told him about rock soup. Brer Fox, he was no fool. He was a smart one and he saw through the thing right off. But he didn't let Brer Rabbit see that he suspected anything. He told Brer Rabbit to go right ahead and make the rock soup.

Brer Fox handed Brer Rabbit whatever was called for— meat, vegetables, seasoning. When the soup was done, it tasted like any other soup Brer Fox had ever tasted.

When the soup was eaten up, Brer Fox took the rock from the bottom of the pot and threw it down his well. "There, now it can make soup down there," said Brer Fox to Brer Rabbit. But, of course, all that came up was plain drinking water. That made all the family laugh at Brer Rabbit and he was so ashamed, he loped off. It was a long time before he dared show his face at Brer Fox's place. And he never did find another rock to make soup.

Brer Rabbit and Brer Fox are both very cunning but that time Brer Fox got the better of Brer Rabbit, for sure.

The Little Red House
By Carolyn Sherwin Bailey

The author was a prolific story writer and collector in the early decades of the 20th century. Unfortunately, she rarely gave an indication of the sources of her inspiration. This story, adapted from a text she first wrote down some 80 years ago, was almost surely inspired by Central European folk customs surrounding the apple. The tale became widely used among Sunday school teachers in North America, was then almost forgotten, and of late has been revived, mostly through oral retellings by kindergarten teachers. Of course, after telling it, one must always share an apple, cut so that the audience can look at the star.

Once upon a time there was a little boy who was tired of all his old toys and all his old playthings and all his old picture books.

"What shall I do?" he asked his mother, and she, who always knew beautiful things for little boys to do, said,

"Go and find a little red house with no windows and no doors and a beautiful star inside. Down the lane, past the farmer's house, and over the hill," said his mother. "Come back as soon as you can tell me all about your journey."

So the boy started out. He had not gone very far down the lane when he came to a little girl, dancing along in the sunshine.

"Do you know where I can find a little red house with no windows and no doors and a beautiful star inside?" he asked her.

The little girl laughed. "I know where there is a red barn, but it is big. Ask my father, the farmer," she said.

So the boy went on until he came to the great red barn, where the farmer himself stood in the doorway.

"Do you know where I can find a little red house with no windows and no doors and a beautiful star inside?" asked the boy.

The farmer shook his head. "I have lived a great many years and I have never seen such a house. But ask Grannie, who lives at the foot of the hill. She knows how to make candy and popcorn balls and red mittens. Perhaps she can direct you."

So the boy went on farther still until he came to Grannie's house. She was sitting in front of her house, knitting a red mitten.

"Please, dear Grannie," asked the boy, "where will I find a little red house with no windows and no doors and a beautiful star inside?"

Grannie paused in her knitting and laughed cheerily. "I should like to find that little red house myself," she chuckled. "It would be warm on frosty nights. Starlight is more pleasant than any other light. Ask the wind who blows about so much and listens in at the chimney. Perhaps the wind can direct you to the little red house with no windows and no doors and with the beautiful star inside."

The boy took off his hat, bowed politely to Grannie, and went to climb the hill. At the bottom of the hill, he met the wind. It turned around and went winging along beside him. It whistled in his ear.

After they had gone together for quite a way, the boy asked, "Wind, can you help me find a little red house with no windows and no doors and a beautiful star inside?"

The wind cannot speak in words, but it went whipping along ahead of the boy until it came to an apple tree. The wind shook the branch just as the boy arrived at the top of the hill, and there lay a rosy apple at his feet. It was as red as the sun had been able to paint it, and a thick brown stem stood up on top, like a chimney. Could it be that this was the little red house with no windows and no doors?

"I wonder. . ." thought the little boy. He took out his pocketknife and cut the apple through the center. There, inside the apple, lay a star holding the brown seeds. The boy called "Thank you" to the wind, and the wind whistled back, "You're welcome."

The boy ran home to his mother and gave her the apple. "It is too wonderful to eat without looking at the star," he said.

"Yes, indeed," said his mother.

America
South of the Rio Grande

Juan Tonto
Translated and adapted by Anne Pellowski

Many countries have stories about young men or women who appear to be foolish and silly on the outside but who are really very clever in the end. In English, these tales are usually about a character called Jack. In Spanish, he is called Juan Bobo or Juan Tonto. "Foolish Juan" stories can be found throughout Latin America. This one is a riddle story from Juanacatlan, Jalisco.

There was once a young man who lived on a farm, and he was so foolish that all the neighbors called him Juan Tonto. One day the king published an announcement: "If there is some young man in the kingdom who can ask my daughter, the princess, a riddle that she cannot answer, that person may marry the princess. But if the princess does answer the riddle, the person asking it will pay with his life."

Many young men arrived at the royal palace to try their hand at posing riddles, but the princess answered all of them, and the king had them all executed.

One day, Juan Tonto said to his mother, "I am going to the palace to pose a riddle to the princess, a riddle she will not be able to answer."

"Oh, no," said his mother. "Please don't go." But Juan Tonto felt he must, so off he went to the palace. It took him many days to get there, but as soon as he arrived, he asked the princess the following riddle:

"Foundation on top of foundation; foundation on top of foundation;
On top of the foundations is a box;

On top of the box is a cross;
On top of the cross is a mill;
On top of the mill are two caves;
On top of the caves are two lights;
On top of the lights is a hill;
On top of the hill are some trees;
And in the trees are some thieves.
Let's see if you can guess what that is!"

The princess thought and thought but she could not guess the answer, so Juan Tonto explained it to her:

"The lower foundations are my feet; the upper foundations are my legs. The box is my body. The cross is made by my arms when I hold them wide like this. The mill is my mouth. The two caves are my nostrils. The two lights are my eyes. The hill is my head, and the trees are my hair." Juan Tonto paused.

"And the thieves?" asked the princess.

Juan Tonto laughed: "The thieves are the lice in my hair, because I haven't had a bath since I left home. Now, can we get married?"

So Juan Tonto had a bath and he married the princess.

Gammon and the Woman's Tongue Tree
By Diane Browne

In many parts of the world, if plants have the same shape as certain parts of the human body, they are named for that body part. In Jamaica, one kind of laburnam tree is called the woman's tongue tree because the leaves are shaped like a human tongue. Men's tongues have the same shape as women's so why is the tree named only after women? Probably because it was commonly believed that women talked and gossiped more than men. Women were often made fun of for this reason. But social scientists have shown that when averaged out, men and women talk about the same amount. Perhaps in the future, Jamaicans and others will call this tree simply the tongue tree. But regardless of what it is called, this tree provokes a funny mystery in this story from Jamaica. The word *ackee* (p. 147) is a kind of fruit. The phrase "in his ackee" is the equivalent of "he is in clover."

Gammon was a little goat that belonged to Farmer Joe. He looked like any other little goat with his brown hairy coat, but Gammon was lazy. He hated to have to wander around for food like the other goats, and so at every opportunity he would find a shady spot and go to sleep.

One day when Gammon was feeling especially lazy, he left the other goats that were grazing along the roadside and looked for somewhere to rest. He soon found a big woman's tongue tree, which only months before had been bare of leaves, and its long brown pods had clattered loudly in the breeze. But the rains had come; and now the tree was covered with bright green leaves and lovely feathery flowers, which ranged from pale lime-yellow to deep mustard-yellow. It was dark and cool beneath the tree, and in no time at all Gammon had fallen asleep in the thick green grass.

The sun was just setting when Gammon awoke. He opened his eyes; then he shut them tightly again. He peeped through his pale eyelashes and blinked. Around him stood a crowd of children. Gammon was sure they would stone him, for amongst them were some of the naughtiest children in the village. His heart thumped in his little chest as he wondered how he would escape.

Then Gammon realized that the children were pointing and exclaiming in surprise: "What a sweet little goat! What a lovely yellow goat! What a pretty golden goat!"

Gammon looked around for this strange goat that they were talking about, but there was no other goat to be seen. Then as he turned his head from side to side, he caught sight of his own hairy coat. He could not believe his eyes. He was covered in fine yellow hairs and tight little mustard-colored balls. Gammon did not know what had happened to him, and at first he was frightened. But soon he became as excited as the children by his new coat.

Delighted by his appearance, Gammon set out for home to show off his coat to the other goats. The excited children followed him, calling out, "Golden goat! Golden goat!"

All along the way they were followed by people who were amazed to see such a strange-looking goat. So when Gammon got to Farmer Joe's yard, he had a long line of chattering people behind him. The news of the golden goat had even spread to the village, and by the time Farmer Joe appeared to find out what was happening, there was an astonished crowd at his gate pushing and boring as they tried to catch sight of Gammon. Gammon was surprised that Farmer Joe did not seem to recognize him.

"Is this your goat, Mass Joe?" asked Brother Caleb, a man who made things from goatskins. "I've never seen such a goat as this before. People say is a golden goat. Where you get him from?"

Gammon could not believe his ears when he heard Farmer Joe answer, "Is a special goat, Brother Caleb. Is not from around here; in fact, is a foreign goat."

Well, at the mention of the word *foreign* a ripple of excitement went through the crowd. They were convinced that they were seeing a real golden goat from another country. . . .

Farmer Joe seemed to be as pleased as Gammon was to be the center of attraction, but he quickly led him away from the curious crowd and into the yard. "Ah," said Farmer Joe when he was sure no one could hear him. "This goat come to my yard. So I will keep it. And if it really is a golden goat, what a thing to take to the Agricultural Fair."

Meanwhile, the other goats who had gathered when they heard the noise, stared at Gammon. They recognized him, though they couldn't imagine what had happened to him. They were longing to ask him, but Farmer Joe did not give them the chance. He locked Gammon securely in the shed where he usually put his ground provisions. Gammon realized that Farmer Joe wanted to keep him safe for the night.

The other goats returned to their pen and crowded around their three most respected members to discuss the matter.

"It looks like Gammon, but are we sure it is Gammon?" said Delores Goat, sniffing anxiously. She was feeling a bit annoyed. She was famous because she had one totally black kid with a white foreleg, and one totally white kid with a black hind leg. Everyone said that these kids would win the prize at the Agricultural Fair. But Delores was not sure now that people were making such a fuss over the golden goat. So irritable was she that she shooed away the two kids, who were trying to nestle against her, and sniffed again.

"I'm sure," replied Inez Goat, who was famous for her milk. Inez had nursed many kids whose mothers could not feed them, and even people bought her milk for their children. "I must know Gammon," she said, "I fed him when he was very little."

The goats turned to Simon, the wise old goat, who was famous because he had seen everything and heard everything in his travels. Simon Goat had climbed up and down the mountains, from the Blue Mountains in the East to the Dolphin Head Mountains in the West. "What do you think?" they asked. "Have you heard of a goat changing color like that? Have you ever seen a golden goat?"

Simon Goat shook his long hairy beard and said, "I have never, not in all my travels from the Blue Mountains to the East to the Dolphin Head Mountains in the West."

"Maybe it is a foreign goat, and not Gammon at all," said Delores Goat, rubbing her nose, which was beginning to itch, against a fence post. "Perhaps they have golden goats in other countries. You have only traveled in Jamaica, Simon. You don't know everything," she added sharply.

"Well," replied Simon calmly, "there was once a story about a ram's golden fleece, but I am sure that was only a story. I tell you, there is no such thing as a golden goat. Things are not always what they seem to be. Mark my words!"

"And besides," said Inez Goat firmly, "it is Gammon. I must know Gammon."

Life changed for Gammon after that. At night he slept in the cosy shed; in the daytime Farmer Joe cut guinea grass and the branches of acacia trees and brought them for him to eat. Gammon did not have to do anything. He did not have to wander around with the other goats nibbling at the bright croton bushes or prickly privet. He did not have to look out for the dangerous twists of orange love-bush that twirled across many of the hedges. But there was one thing that Gammon did. He always rested in the heat of the day under one of the many woman's tongue trees with their yellow blossoms.

Simon Goat noticed this and stroked his long hairy beard thoughtfully, but he just said wisely, "This is only a nine-day wonder, like everything else. Mark my words!"

Delores Goat was annoyed by Simon's calm attitude. She became increasingly upset the more she thought about the Agricultural Fair. She did not even want to see her totally black kid and her totally white kid. She just walked around sniffing and blowing her nose.

Inez Goat thought that Delores was being very silly. But when Farmer Joe removed the sign on his gate which said:

BEST GOAT MILK FOR SALE
$1.00 A PINT

she couldn't believe it. And when he replaced it with one which read:

COME AND SEE THE GOLDEN GOAT
ENTRANCE FEE $1.00
CHILDREN   50¢

it was all she could do to stop her milk from going sour.

So people came from far and near to see Gammon the golden goat. They stared at him in wonder. They had never seen such a goat before, but they had all heard that he was from another country so they knew he was a golden goat.

One day when Gammon was tired of showing off for the people who came to see him, he decided to take a walk to the village. All along the way people and children said hello to him politely. In the village people came out of their shops and told him good morning. Gammon was very pleased with himself for most of these people never even bothered to speak to the other goats.

After all, people were too busy going about their work to

speak to goats, but Gammon was different.

When Gammon got to Brother Caleb's shop, he stopped. Brother Caleb had bags and rugs made from goatskins. Even though he never troubled the goats in the village, it sent shivers up and down their legs just to see all those things made from black, white, brown, and gray goat's hair. None of the goats would have stopped to look inside that shop, but now Gammon did, behaving just as if he might buy something. Brother Caleb shook his head in bewilderment and stared at Gammon, but he said nothing. Gammon continued walking until he came to Miss Mattie's shop. Miss Mattie sold cooked food, and in front of her shop was a sign in bold black letters:

Curried Goat Dinners
Sold Here Every Day

None of the other goats ever went near Miss Mattie's shop, for obvious reasons. Moreover, people in the village suspected Miss Mattie when any of their goats disappeared. But Gammon walked right up to the shop, read the sign, tossed his head, and said brazenly, "Maa-aa, Maa-aa."

Miss Mattie was sitting on her stool in front of the shop. Her mouth fell open in astonishment. Then she glared at Gammon, but she was clearly afraid to say anything to a golden goat. So angrily she got up, and swinging her skirt, she kissed her teeth loudly and went inside. Gammon laughed at her. And the people laughed when they saw what had happened.

When Simon Goat heard all this, he said, "Gammon is in his ackee, but nothing lasts forever. Mark my words!"

On the day of the Agricultural Fair, Farmer Joe put Gammon into his little cart. Over the back of the cart he had built a shelter of coconut boughs. Gammon rode, protected from the hot sun and the dry wind, while behind walked the other goats. The wheels of the cart stirred up the dust from the powdery road. It swirled around the goats' heads and settled on their coats. It was soon obvious that none of them could enter the competition at the fair, not even Delores Goat's kids. The white kid was becoming totally beige, and the black kid was becoming totally gray. Delores could not even bear to look at them.

At last the little band reached the fair grounds. People came running from all sides to get a look at the golden goat under the coconut boughs in the back of the little cart. Many had come from miles around just to see such a goat.

All kinds of goats were waiting to see who would win the prize. There were gray goats, brown goats, black goats, and white goats, but there was only one golden goat.

The wind whipped across the open field as the various goats and their owners began to parade in front of the judges. It whisked the dust into spirals, tossing leaves and twigs into the air. It ruffled the goats' hairy coats.

When it was Gammon's turn, he moved with almost a cantering gait, his head held high. He felt the wind tickle his nostrils; it brushed against his eyelashes. Gammon felt it lifting the hairs on his coat.

A gasp went up from the large crowd. Yellow fluff and golden strands swirled into the air. The people wondered if a golden breeze was blowing. Then as the wind dropped, they looked again at the golden goat.

But instead, there stood Gammon, the same little brown goat he had been before he became a golden goat. There was not one little golden hair left on him, not even one little yellow strand.

Delores Goat was so astonished that she stopped sniffing at once. Inez Goat was so shocked that it was all she could do to stop her milk from going sour. And Simon Goat said, "I told you to mark my words," as he threw back his head and laughed.

Slowly it dawned on the people that Gammon had never

been a golden goat but was really only covered by yellow blossoms from a woman's tongue tree; he had never been a foreign goat but was really only Gammon himself.

There was a terrible uproar. Some people pointed at Farmer Joe and held their sides as they roared with laughter; but others shook their fists in anger as they realized how they had been fooled. Some of them started across the field towards Farmer Joe, but in their anxiety to get to him they bumped into one another. And in all the pushing and pulling and tumbling around, Farmer Joe and Gammon escaped from the fair.

Farmer Joe was so embarrassed that he went to stay in another part of the island, leaving Simon Goat in charge of the farm. He was never heard from again, and so Simon Goat eventually inherited the farm. As for Gammon, after all that excitement he decided that village life was too quiet for him, and besides he felt it was best for him to leave; so he went to the North Coast and got a job at one of the hotels where there was goat-racing.

Now when Gammon is not working hard racing in the sand, he rests in the shade of the almond or sea-grape trees. But he never goes near the woman's tongue trees, unless they are bare of leaves and their long brown pods clatter in the breeze.

Casi Lampu'a Lentemue
Retold by Pura Belpre

For many years, Pura Belpre told stories for the New York Public Library system. She wrote down many of her stories, but this version of an old favorite tale is recorded here as I remember her telling it. The verse should be sung and the simple tune can be found in the companion volume to this collection, *A World of Children's Songs.*

Once upon a time, in a village in Puerto Rico, there lived a poor woman named Rosa and her only son, Paco. One day she gave him some money and sent him off to the city to buy some olive oil.

It was a hot summer day. Paco wore his big straw hat to keep the sun out of his eyes, but he was soon very tired and thirsty. By and by he came to a short path that branched off from the road. At the end of the path he could see a small house, surrounded by a grove of thick, shady trees. And was that the sound of rippling water he heard? Paco decided to walk down the short path toward the house, and to have a siesta under one of the trees.

What a surprise! There, sitting under one of the trees, was a very old woman.

"*Buenos dias*, Paco," she said. "You look hot and tired. Come into my house and have a *refresco*, a cooling drink."

Paco stared at her. She looked so very old, and yet, he seemed to see a merry twinkle in her eyes. So he followed her into the house.

She gave him some *refresco*—one, two, three cups. Then, thanking the old woman, Paco walked to the door and tried to open it to leave. It was locked! He turned around. There, in a corner of the room, sitting on a high stool, was the old woman laughing.

Poor Paco! He cried and begged to be allowed to go, but the old woman only laughed.

"Paco," she said, "no one who enters my house ever leaves it without having had a chance to guess my name. You will also have three chances. If you fail, you must remain with me and work for me forever; but if you guess it, you shall be free. Tomorrow you will start your work in the forest, helping to gather wood."

So the next day Paco went with her into the forest to gather wood. When they returned, the old woman asked him what her name was.

"Margarita," said Paco.

"No," said the old woman, "it is not Margarita."

"Can it be Gabriela?"

"No, it is not Gabriela."

"Esperanza, perhaps?"

"No, it is not Esperanza," said the old woman, and she laughed at him. "You have two more chances, Paco. Tomorrow you must go out and help me gather plants and roots, for medicine."

The next day, Paco went out and helped the old woman gather plants and roots. When their baskets were full they returned to the little house.

"Well, Paco, do you know my name now?" asked the old woman.

"Is it Dolores?"

"No, it is not Dolores."

"Mercedes, perhaps?"

"No, it is not Mercedes."

"Can it be Isabel?"

"No, it is not Isabel. One more chance, Paco. Tomorrow you must fill the cistern that stands in the middle of my patio with water from the river. I will keep watch as you do it."

The next day she gave Paco a pail and sent him down to the river. Paco filled it with water and then returned to empty it into the cistern in the patio. Finally, the cistern was almost full, and Paco realized he must soon make his last guesses. He went back to the river and set the pail on the ground. He sat down on a big rock at the edge of the water, covered his face with his hands, and began to cry.

Suddenly he heard a noise. He looked up and saw a huge red crab, waving both its claws.

"What are you doing here, little boy, and why are you crying?"

"Because today is my last chance," said Paco.

"Your last chance for what?" asked the crab.

"To guess the name of the old woman up there."

"Well, Paco, if that is all, I think I can help you," said the crab. "I can tell you her name, but you must promise not to let her know who told you."

"I promise," said Paco.

"Her name," whispered the crab, "is Casi Lampu'a Lentemue."

"Casi Lampu'a Lentemue," repeated Paco. e took his pail and started back to the house.

"Don't forget," called the crab. "You are not to tell who told you."

When Paco reached the patio, the old woman was waiting for him.

"Well, Paco, what is my name?"

"Luisa," said Paco.

"No, it is not Luisa."

"Elisa," said Paco.

"No, it is not Elisa."

Then Paco looked her right in the eyes. "Your name," he said, "is Casi Lampu'a Lentemue."

When the old woman heard that, she was furious, but before she could ask him any questions, Paco was out of the house, running down the path. He did not stop until he was on the main road, heading toward home. When he looked back, he was just in time to see the old woman disappear into the forest.

The old woman cut a stout stick and then she set off to find out who had told Paco her name. Soon she came to a meadow, and there stood a cow munching grass. The old woman went up to the cow and sang:

"Vaquita, mi esperanza y mi juez,	"Little cow, my hope and my judge,
Vaquita, mi esperanza y mi juez,	Little cow, my hope and my judge,
Dijiste tu que me llamo,	Did you say that my name is
Casi Lampu'a Lentmue?	Casi Lampu'a Lentemue?
Casi Lampu'a Lentemue?"	Casi Lampu'a Lentemue?"

The cow looked at her, shook its head, and answered:

"No soy tu esperanza ni tu juez,	"I am not your hope nor your judge,
No soy tu esperanza ni tu juez,	I am not your hope nor your judge,
Y no he dicho que te llamas,	Nor did I say that your name is
Casi Lampu'a Lentemue.	Casi Lampu'a Lentemue.
Casi Lampu'a Lentemue."	Casi Lampu'a Lentemue."

"But old mother," said the cow, "go on a little further until you meet the goat. She travels over hills and mountains and perhaps she can tell you."

So the old woman went on. By and by she came to the goat. She sang:

"Cabrita, mi esperanza y mi juez,	"Little goat, my hope and my judge,

Cabrita, mi esperanza y mi juez,	Little goat, my hope and my judge,
Dijiste tu que me llamo	Did you say that my name is
Casi Lampu'a Lentemue?	Casi Lampu'a Lentemue?
Casi Lampu'a Lentemue?"	Casi Lampu'a Lentemue?"

The goat answered:

"No soy tu esperanza ni tu juez,	"I am not your hope nor your judge,
No soy tu esperanza ni tu juez,	I am not your hope nor your judge,
Y no he dicho que te llamas	Nor did I say that your name is
Casi Lampu'a Lentemue,	Casi Lampu'a Lentemue,
Casi Lampu'a Lentemue."	Casi Lampu'a Lentemue."

"But, old mother," said the goat, "go on a little further until you come to the pig. She is very wise. Perhaps she can tell you."

The old woman went on her way until she came to a clearing in the woods. There she saw a fat gray pig. She asked her:

"Puerquita, mi esperanza y mi juez,	Little pig, my hope and my judge,
Puerquita, mi esperanza y mi juez,	Little pig, my hope and my judge,
Dijiste tu que me llamo	Did you say that my name is
Casi Lampu'a Lentemue?	Casi Lampu'a Lentemue?
Casi Lampu'a Lentemue?"	Casi Lampu'a Lentemue?"

But the pig replied:

"No soy tu esperanza ni tu juez,	"I am not your hope nor your judge,
No soy tu esperanza ni tu juez,	I am not your hope nor your judge,

Y no he dicho que te llamas	Nor did I say that your name is
Casi Lampu'a Lentemue,	Casi Lampu'a Lentemue,
Casi Lampu'a Lentemue."	Casi Lampu'a Lentemue."

"Old mother," said the pig, " go down by the river and find the crab. He may be able to tell you."

So the old woman went to the river. She was tired, so she sat down on a rock. Suddenly she saw a huge crab come out from under the rock. She called out to the crab:

"Juey, mi esperanza y mi juez,	"Little crab, my hope and my judge,
Juey, mi esperanza y mi juez,	Little crab, my hope and my judge,
Dijiste tu que me llamo	Did you say that my name is
Casi Lampu'a Lentemue?	Casi Lampu'a Lentemue?
Casi Lampu'a Lentemue?"	Casi Lampu'a Lentemue?"

The crab looked at her in surprise, and then he replied:

"Si, soy tu esperanza y tu juez,	"Yes, I am your hope and your judge,
Si, soy tu esperanza y tu juez,	Yes, I am your hope and your judge,
Y yo dije que tu te llamas	And I did say that your name is
Casi Lampu'a Lentemue,	Casi Lampu'a Lentemue,
Casi Lampu'a Lentemue."	Casi Lampu'a Lentemue."

When the old woman heard that she raised her stick and wanted to beat the crab. But he scampered under the rock as fast as he could. And that is why, even today, crabs run and hide when they see a human being, out of fear that it is a descendant of the old woman looking for them.

Yes or No: A Story Hidden in an Old Book

By Gaby de Bolivar
Translated by Anne Pellowski

The author wrote this story to honor the memory of Mrs. Jella Lepman, founder of the International Youth Library in Munich, Germany, and of the organization known as IBBY, the International Board on Books for Young People. Mrs. Lepman believed that it was through good children's literature that peaceful and cooperative lives could be nourished among all peoples.

There was once an old book with dry, yellow pages. It was hidden away in a dusty corner. Each night the book dreamed a horrible dream. In the dream a child would come along and tear out one of its pages. The book cried each time upon awakening. During the day it simply stood there, mute and frightened by the dream of the previous night.

But one day, something different happened. The small hands of a little girl lifted it up, dusted it off, opened the pages, and began to read:

"There was once a king who was always fighting wars. He usually won the wars, but suddenly he noticed that each time he won a war, a piece of his heart was eaten up. Soon, he would have no heart left in his body. He also discovered that the young men who had died in the wars also had had their hearts partly eaten away. Disturbed, the king went around his kingdom and discovered that there were no longer any theaters, or musicians, or people playing games. But worst of all,

in all the chambers of the palace, everything had disappeared except swords, shields, arquebuses, and armor. He went out in the streets and noticed that the children were no longer eating any fruits or sweets. The women walked around with sad faces. When he returned to the palace, the king noticed that his wife, too, had lost her sweet smile. So, he decided to walk off toward the open horizon. He walked for three nights and three days, thinking and thinking. On the third day, he suddenly shouted, 'No! No more war. I want to have peace.' And suddenly, everything seemed clear to him."

When the little girl finished reading the story, the book realized that it had not been part of a dream. The story of the king was written on its pages. The girl told the story to many of her friends, and they told it to their friends. The book passed from hand to hand, and it was printed in many languages until all the children of the world had read it. And from that moment on, things began to get clearer and better.

The Singing Frog
Translated by Anne Pellowski

This traditional cumulative tale is as widely known throughout the Spanish-speaking parts of the Americas as "The House That Jack Built" and "The Old Woman and Her Pig" are in English-speaking lands. In some cases it is sung and in others it is recited in a kind of chant. For a Mexican version with music see *A World of Children's Songs*.

There once was a frog sitting in the water and singing.
When the frog went out to sing
Along came the fly and said, "Be quiet!"
Fly on the frog, sitting in the water and singing.
When the fly went out to sing
Along came the spider and said, "Be quiet!"
Spider on the fly, fly on the frog,
    sitting in the water and singing.

When the spider went out to sing
Along came the rat and said, "Be quiet!"
Rat on the spider, spider on the fly, fly on the frog,
    sitting in the water and singing.
When the rat went out to sing
Along came the cat and said, "Be quiet!"
Cat on the rat, rat on the spider, spider on the fly,
    fly on the frog, sitting in the water and singing.

When the cat went out to sing
Along came the dog and said, "Be quiet!"

Dog on the cat, cat on the rat, rat on the spider,
    spider on the fly, fly on the frog, sitting in the water
    and singing.

When the dog went out to sing
Along came the stick and said, "Be quiet!"
Stick on the dog, dog on the cat, cat on the rat,
    rat on the spider, spider on the fly, fly on the frog,
    sitting in the water and singing.

When the stick went out to sing
Along came the fire and said, "Be quiet!"
Fire on the stick, stick on the dog, dog on the cat,
    cat on the rat, rat on the spider, spider on the fly,
    fly on the frog, sitting in the water and singing.

When the fire went out to sing
Along came the water and said, "Be quiet!"
Water on the fire, fire on the stick, stick on the dog,
    dog on the cat, cat on the rat, rat on the spider,
    spider on the fly, fly on the frog,
    sitting in the water and singing.

When the water went out to sing
Along came the girl (boy, woman, man) and said, "Be quiet!"
Girl on the water, water on the fire, fire on the stick,
    stick on the dog, dog on the cat, cat on the rat,
    rat on the spider, spider on the fly, fly on the frog,
    sitting in the water and singing.

When the girl went out to sing
No one could tell her, "Be quiet!"
It was she who taught me this song, and that is why I can
    sing it:

Girl on the water, water on the fire, fire on the stick,
 stick on the dog, dog on the cat, cat on the rat,
 rat on the spider, spider on the fly, fly on frog,
 sitting in the water and singing.

Oceania

I Am Forgiven
By Mariana Tinggal

We have all, at one time or another, probably hurt another person by doing something wrong. This young writer, who is from the Kadazan people of Malaysia, feels she was lucky because she had a chance to say she was sorry, and to be forgiven. The rambutan tree in this story is of the soapberry family; it bears juicy, red, egg-shaped fruit.

Mr. Oldie lived alone. He worked as a rubber tapper. He was a tall, dark-skinned man. The wrinkles on his forehead showed his age. But Mr. Oldie was still strong and muscular.

During the fruit season, his garden became a paradise for naughty children, who went in to steal the ripe, juicy fruit. If Mr. Oldie caught the children, he would sometimes tie them to a rambutan tree until he, the children's parents, and the village headman had decided on their punishment.

One day my friend Salina and I decided to take some fruit from Mr. Oldie's garden. We saw that no one was there, not even Mr. Oldie. I started to climb, my eyes wild with excitement, looking for the red, ripe rambutan fruit. My mouth watered. I plucked one and skinned it with my teeth. I squealed with pleasure, it was so delicious.

"Sssh!" Salina warned me. I looked down at her below. With one hand she was sucking on a juicy rambutan fruit, while her alert eyes surveyed the grounds on her left and right. The nimble fingers of her other hand were filling her school bag with fruit.

"Hey! The bag is full," Salina broke the silence. We quickly ran off. We hid behind a bush near my house, waiting for the other children to come back from school so my parents would not know that I had not gone to school. As soon as we heard the children returning, Salina ran off, and I turned toward my own home.

"Thief! Thief!"

Where did the voice come from?

"Thief! Thief! Where is the thief. I want to cut him in pieces!"

My ears heard. My heart understood. It was Mr. Oldie. My heart beat faster.

"I'll die," my heart whispered to me.

Mr. Oldie came out from his back door. I ran away, still seeing the long knife that Mr. Oldie had been holding. "What will it feel like if he cuts me to pieces?" I wondered.

I ran to Salina's house. "We'll die, Lina. . . . Mr. Oldie— he's mad—he was holding a knife," I stammered.

Salina's face turned pale, then red, then pale again. Her eyes almost popped out as she stared right into my eyes.

"Let's go and hide." Salina pulled my hand.

We ran to a swampy area with many palm trees, with bushy areas below. We looked through the holes we found in the shrubs. Salina and I could see our village from the hideout.

"There . . ." Salina pointed.

We saw Mr. Oldie talking with the village headman. Mr. Oldie's long knife swayed to and fro as if he were cutting something. We waited a long time before we went back home. It was already getting dark.

"Mr. Oldie came to complain. Children from this village stole his rambutan. Don't you be naughty like them!" my father sternly warned me. "Naughty children will be burnt in hell," Father continued.

That night I could not sleep. The adventure had been exciting but frightening. "What will happen if they discover that I am the real thief?" I asked myself.

A day passed. Then two days. I still felt uneasy. Finally, I had a plan.

I went to see Salina, who did not like the plan. But she did agree to accompany me to go out and meet Mr. Oldie.

Mr. Oldie's house was quiet. It was still early in the morning. Salina called out: "Mr. Oldie!"

Mr. Oldie came out of the house. He was not smiling in welcome.

"Mr. Oldie . . . I came to say sorry . . . actually, we were the ones who stole your rambutan two days ago, . . ." I stammered, still trembling.

Mr. Oldie did not say a word. He looked straight at us, first me and then Salina. But he still did not say anything.

"Is Mr. Oldie going to cut me into pieces?" I asked myself, not daring to speak aloud. I looked at Mr. Oldie's hands. There was no long knife in them.

Slowly, Mr. Oldie came down the steps of his house. I did not dare move an inch. He took a long pole into his hands. I became more frightened.

Then Mr. Oldie walked right past us into his garden. He poked at the fruit in the rambutan tree with his long pole. It was the same tree I had climbed two days earlier. Four bunches of fruit dropped to the ground.

"I am impressed with your courage, children," Mr. Oldie said, and he smiled. "Here. Take these fruits. I forgive you."

Since that day, I never stole again.

-169-

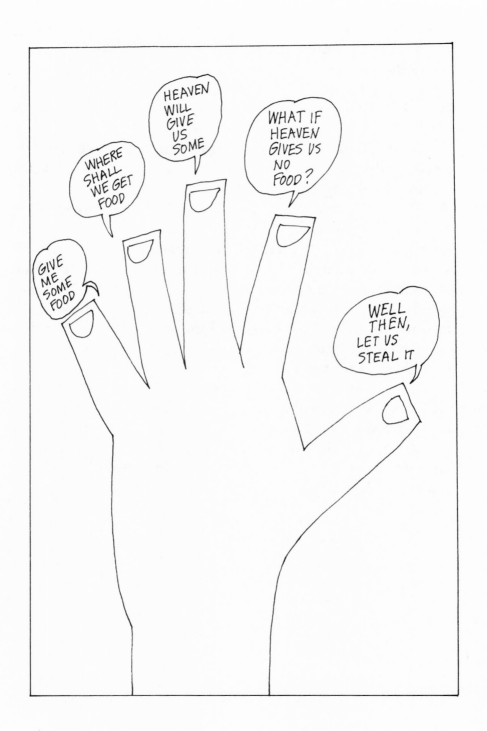

The Story of Our Fingers
Retold by Leopoldo Uichanco
Translated by Dean Fansler

Stories about the parts of the body and why they are shaped the way they are can be found in many parts of the world, but they are less common than origin stories about plant or animal shapes. This is a Tagalog version of a tale explaining the relationship of the fingers to the thumb.

In the Philippines a common finger rhyme goes like this:

Maya-mayang saday	Pretty little sparrow (little finger)
Magayon na singsingan	Beautiful for a ring (ring finger)
Daculang mangmang	Long but lazy fellow (middle finger)
Atrevido	Insolent thing (index finger)
Hababang tao	Dumpy, dwarfish one (thumb)

Why does our thumb stand separate from the other fingers?

That is so only in our day. In the days of long ago the fingers of our ancestors stood together in the same position. One day one of these fingers, the one we call little finger, became very hungry, and he asked the finger next to him to give him some food.

"Oh, Brother!" said the ring finger in reply. I am hungry too; but where shall we get food?"

"Heaven is merciful," put in the middle finger as he tried to comfort his two brothers. "Heaven will give us some."

"But Brother Middle Finger," protested the index finger, "what if heaven gives us no food?"

"Well then," interrupted the thumb, "let us steal it."

"Steal!" echoed the index finger. He was not at all pleased at the advice that had just been given. "You know better than to do that, I hope."

"Yes, that is a bad policy," agreed the other three unanimously. "Your idea is against morality, against God, against yourself, against everybody. Our conscience will not permit us to steal."

"Oh, no, you are greatly mistaken, my friends!" said the thumb angrily. "How can you call my plan bad policy when it can save your lives and mine?"

"Well, if that is your plan," said the other four fingers, "you can go your own way and we will go ours. We would rather starve than steal." And the four fingers would have nothing further to do with thumb.

So that is why we see our thumbs separated from the other fingers. He wanted to be a thief, and they did not care to live with him. And because the finger we call little finger did not get enough to eat in those days, it remains small and weak right to this very day.

How the Land Snail Got His Shell
Retold by Tekeraoi Beneati

In many parts of the Pacific, turtles grow to be very large and very old. They move about slowly and seem to think before they move. They are thought to have great wisdom and patience, much like the owl in European and American folk-lore. Therefore, in folktales from the Pacific region the turtle is the animal who "knows the answers."

Long, long ago Beach Crab and Land Snail were the only creatures besides birds on these islands. At first they were very friendly and lived together. Beach Crab could run fast and catch nearly everything he saw, but Land Snail could only walk slowly, keeping off sharp stones, because he had no shell in those days.

Every day Beach Crab went fishing while Land Snail collected food from the land. Land Snail worked well and honestly, but Beach Crab ate most of the fish himself. He gave only a small piece to his friend. One day all the food from the land was finished. Land Snail could find nothing to eat. Beach Crab laughed behind him.

Days went by and Land Snail became thinner and weaker. Beach Crab still got his food from the sea, waiting for Land Snail to die. Then he would be owner of the island.

Land Snail became too weak to walk. He lay under a stone, thinking. Suddenly, he remembered the cleverest creature, Turtle, who knew both the land and the sea. Without delay Land Snail crawled with effort to the southern tip of the island where Turtle came, at full moon, to lay her eggs.

At last he found her, but Land Snail was too tired to speak. He bent his head and tried to catch his breath. Turtle waited and looked at him in pity. At last Land Snail told Turtle his story.

"Why don't you find your food in the sea?" said Turtle.

"I'm afraid that the fish will snap at my soft stomach," replied Land Snail.

"All right," said Turtle, "I have seen many empty shells in the sea that will fit you, and because you are honest and humble, I will fetch you one. When that shell becomes too small, then you can go to the sea yourself and get a new one. "

Turtle went to the sea and found a beautiful shell. Land Snail happily tried it on, thanking Turtle many times. As he left for home, Turtle said: "Be honest and humble and you will be liked and respected. Your bad friend Beach Crab will be disliked by everyone he meets."

As Land Snail neared home, Beach Crab saw him. He could not believe his eyes. He stared at Land Snail for a long time. He became ashamed at what he had done to his friend, so he dug a hole in the sand and hid in it.

Background Notes

These notes give information about the sources of the stories and some tips for telling them or reading them aloud. I have indicated the present occupation of those authors who are still living, where it was possible. Every effort has been made to reach copyright holders. It was not always possible.

Asia East of the Caspian

The Mouse Bride - INDIA

This version combines the Theodor Benfey translation (1859) and the Arthur W. Ryder translation (1956). The Sanskrit original has both prose sections and long segments of verse. Many of the verses, however, are filled with allusions to Hindu and Buddhist scriptures, so it is difficult to translate them meaningfully without adding copious notes. But I have tried to leave in at least a few verses, so as to give a touch of the original style.

The Naughty Frog - MYANMAR (BURMA)

This tale is taken from an article on the cumulative tale, found in the *Journal of the Burmese Research Society* (1914). A writer who has very successfully adapted this format to modern cumulative tales is Bill Martin, Jr., in his books *Brown Bear, Brown Bear, What Do You See?* (1983) and *Polar Bear, Polar Bear, What Do You Hear?* (1991).

At the Edge of the Sky - HMONG

This chant is adapted from the texts given by David Crockett Graham in *Songs and Stories of the Ch'uan Miao* (Smithsonian

Institution, Miscellaneous Collections 123, 1954). These people are called Miao by the Chinese but call themselves Hmong. More than 100,000 Hmong now live in the United States. These chants are better when read aloud or recited by two persons. Another good source of Hmong stories, especially those told in their story cloths, is *Folk Stories of the Hmong* by Norma Livo and Dia Cha (1991).

I Don't Want to Be a Buffalo - THAILAND

This story is reprinted from *The Story: Reading Animation Seminar, Bangkok* (1991). The author is a cabinet minister in the government of Thailand, working for the rights of women and children in that country. She is also affiliated with the Thai section of the International Board on Books for Young People (IBBY). The translator is also a supporter of Thai IBBY. "Mom Rajawong," which precedes her name, refers to a rank related to the royal family of Thailand.

The Rabbit and the Moon - THAILAND

This story is reprinted from *The Story: Reading Animation Seminar, Bangkok* (1991). The author is a teacher in Thailand. If you wish to read or tell the Buddhist story of how the rabbit got to the moon, you can find it in almost any collection of Jataka tales. A modern variant, using a candle, paper, and lemon juice to show the mystery of the rabbit figure in the moon, can be found in Anne Pellowski, *The Family Storytelling Handbook* (1987).

Rainy Day Drawing Stories - JAPAN

These are my own retellings of two widely known drawing stories as passed down among Japanese children. Before telling these stories, you should practice enough times so that you learn to place the strokes in just the right positions so that the drawing comes out looking reasonably like the animal. There are hundreds of such stories, many of them still not written down. For those who read Japanese, the following source is useful: *Nihon Densho No Asobi Tokumon* (1967).

Middle East

The Alphabet – JEWISH

Louis Ginzberg was born in Lithuania in 1873 and went to the United States in 1899. He became a great scholar and taught for many years at Jewish Theological Seminary in New York. Although he recognized that the Jewish people are chiefly "People of the Book," he was intrigued about the many legends and stories that had been passed down orally but that did not appear in the Bible. Out of his research came many scholarly books, including his seven-volume work, *The Legends of the Jews* (1909-1928). This story is taken from volume 1.

The Prince Who Learned a Profession - EGYPT

I adapted this portion from the Mohammed cycle as it was taken down by Wilhelm Spitta and published in *Contes arabes modernes* (1883). However, in certain details I followed a version told by participants in the children's literature workshop organized by the Integrated Care Society, held in Cairo in 1985.

Mirror Hearts - IRAN

H. Moradi Kermani delivered this story as part of his speech at the 23rd congress of the International Board on Books for Young People (IBBY) in Berlin, September 1992. At that time, he was being honored as a highly commended writer by the Hans Christian Andersen Award jury. He said that his "little people" were his books. He lives in Tehran. Used by permission of the author.

Abou Hadaba - LEBANON

This story was created during a workshop for children's book writers and illustrators of the Arab-speaking world, sponsored by the Kuwait Society for the Advancement of Arab Children, held in Cyprus in 1985. It is used by permission. Because spoken, colloquial Arabic is so different from written, classical Arabic, it is very difficult to write stories that appeal to young children, in language they are able to read themselves. Each of the workshop participants was given the challenge of taking a rhyme or short folktale, commonly known in colloquial language throughout the Arab world, and of transforming it into an appealing story. That is what Rima Khalifeh accomplished with "Abou Hadaba."

Africa South of the Sahara

Bole Gets Dressed - KENYA

I recommend making a set of felt figures for telling this story. Make the Bole figure of dark brown felt, about two feet high. Children love to help in the telling of this story, by placing first the color object on the figure and then replacing it with the correct piece of clothing. At the end of the story, I generally play a game, asking the audience if they can describe things as Bole would, using for colors only names of things from nature and the environment. I ask a few persons who have clothing of an unusual color to stand up, one by one, and we then see if we can find exact matches in something from nature. I explain that it is not enough to say "sky" or "sea" for blue, because the sky and sea have many colors, depending on the time of day, where one is standing, and other variables. The more accurate and exact one can be in such descriptions, the more one is considered to be a fine speaker or linguist. One of the most specific examples of color words in an African language that I have ever heard was in Twi, from Ghana. In that language, when one wishes to refer to a soft, mellow yellow, one says *akoko-sradeE* (pronounced ah-koh-koh-seh-rah-deeyeh), which translates as "chicken-fat color."

This story adapts well to bilingual or trilingual telling. Simply add or substitute at the end phrases such as: *en espanol - blanco*; *en francais - blanche*; *auf deutsch - weiss*; and so on.

The Riot - NIGERIA

Wale Odekiran is a medical doctor, practicing in Ibadan. He is also a writer who is now beginning to write for children, since he believes it is through them that change can come. The story is used by permission. The *galabiya* mentioned in the story is a long, ankle-length garment worn by Muslim men in many parts of Africa. The title *Ma* is a familiar term indicating respect for a woman, usually one who has had children.

Who Is the Cleverest? - ZAIRE

This version is from *Congo Life and Folklore* by John H. Weeks (1911). However, there are many other versions extant, some of which are cited in *African Dilemma Tales* (1975) by William Russell Bascom.

How Anansi Spread Wisdom - GHANA

This Anansi story is my retelling based on oral versions I have heard told by Juliana Sackey of the Ghana Library Board, with some elements taken from the version printed by R. S. Rattray in *Akan-Ashanti Folk Tales* (1930). The song is adapted from a traditional one used by Efua Sutherland in her Children's Theatre Workshop; Ms. Sackey also uses songs like it in many of her storytelling sessions, helping the audience get involved in call and response interludes within the story. I recommend teaching the audience the short refrain, as it appears in *A World of Children's Songs*, a companion volume to this one. Strictly speaking, the teller and the audience interweave the song back and forth in a very intricate rhythmic pattern. I have simplified this procedure by having the teller sing the line and the audience repeat it. *Kra* does not mean "climb" but is meant to indicate the sound made by Anansi as he climbs.

Grasshopper and Toad - MALI

Amadou Dicko is a librarian in the public reading campaign in Mali, known as Operation Lecture Publique. That project has opened up many libraries and reading rooms throughout Mali, where children and young people may read and also share their oral stories. This story is taken from *Les Enfants D'abord* (no. 10, 1992), a grass roots periodical developed in that campaign to allow children, and those who work with them, the opportunity to write down the oral literature they know. Used by permission.

Siime's Handkerchief - TANZANIA

This story was reprinted from an edition published by Uzima Press, Nairobi, and Central Tanganyika Press, Dodoma for DUCCA, a group of African Christian publishers who worked together in producing a series of modern children's stories. Used by permission.

Europe

The Husband and Wife Who Wanted a Child - NETHERLANDS,
OTHER EUROPEAN COUNTRIES

I learned these basic handkerchief figures from Cecile Bejk van Daal and her daughter and aunt, in Eindhoven, Netherlands. In my book *The Family Storytelling Handbook* (1987), I gave directions for the "Babies in the Cradle" figure and pointed out that when Mrs. Bejk van Daal did this figure, she sang a song in Dutch that was a little like "Rock-a-Bye Baby," part sense and part nonsense. This song did not translate well. During the past few years, I have gradually evolved this short story for the figure, and I often use the Mr. and Mrs. Hanky Panky figures to introduce it. When telling the story for an audience of more than five, I recommend placing a large piece of felt on a slanted easel or board. The handkerchief figures cling quite nicely to the felt, and the figures can be seen by the audience. These figures (and others) can be found in a few early printed sources but without any stories. Such sources include the following: *St. Nicholas Magazine* (October 1882); *Out of a Handkerchief* by Frances E. Jacobs (1942); *The Everything Book* by Eleanor Graham Vance (1974). There are other handkerchief stories in *The Family Storytelling Handbook*.

The Little White Rabbit - PORTUGAL

This story is adapted from two versions collected in the 19th century, one by Consiglieri Pedroso, and the other by Francisco Adolpho Coelho. Both were translated by Henriquetta Monteiro in *Tales of Old Lusitania* (1898).

Such stories are fun in and of themselves, but they can also be used as a springboard for discussion about their symbolism. When discussing what kind of people the little rabbit represents, or the little ant, children will often come up with very pertinent social commentary!

The Story of the Water Lily - SERBIA

This translation of Grozdana Olujic's story appeared in *Storytelling Magazine* in spring 1992. The author is a novelist who lives in Belgrade. Some of her books have appeared in English translation. Her fairytales have been translated into almost two dozen languages and sold around the world. The translator of this story, Jascha Kessler, is a professor of English and modern literature at UCLA. He has published eight books of poetry and fiction and six volumes of translations. Used by permission of the author.

The Bear and the Three Granddaughters - POLAND, RUSSIA

This story combines elements from a Polish folktale and from two stories found in the Russian tales collected by Afanasyev: "The Bear and the Old Man's Daughters" and "Snow-girl and the Fox." The Polish tale can be found in A. Steffen's *Jezyk Polskiej Warmii* (1946).

If you wish, you can use nesting dolls to tell the story. Use a five- or six-doll set. Set aside the second-largest doll (and the third-largest, if using the set of six). In that way, there is a nice size differential between grandmother and the three grand-daughters. There are some nesting-doll sets that include the bear, but they are extremely hard to find.

Enough Bread - POLAND

This chant is based on the version found in *Sroczka Kaszke Warzyla* (1918) by Zofia Rogoszowna. There are other variants. When reciting this, I generally like to have the three largest dolls inside each other, and the smallest dolls (three or more—the more the better) either inside each other or lined up. Move one of the child dolls off each time, as though going to the store. Of course, if there is a teeny-tiny doll in the very center, children love it if that doll is the one who brings back the bag of flour. It seems so delightfully incongruous! For more about nesting-doll stories, see *The Story Vine* (1984) and *The Family Storytelling Handbook* (1987).

The Bad Child - SWITZERLAND

This story was translated from *Der Sonntagsvater* (Otto Maier Verlag, 1973) and is used by permission of the author. Eveline Hasler is one of Switzerland's leading writers. Her books have received many national awards, and she has been nominated for the Hans Christian Andersen Award.

America North of the Rio Grande

How Medicine Came to the People - OJIBWAY

This is my retelling based on the texts in Henry Rowe Schoolcraft's *Algic Researches* (1839) and in his *Indian Tribes of the United States*, parts 1 and 5 (1853 and 1856). I also used *Ojibway Texts* collected by William Jones (Publications of the American Ethnological Society, vol. 7, parts 1 and 2, 1917 and 1919). When telling this story, be sure to be aware of the four directions and point them out physically as you come to the part where Otter teaches the people how to find the center. This centering process is a very important part of the belief system of many Native American groups. A modern retelling of this and many other sacred Ojibway stories and customs can be found in *Mishomis*, collected by Edward Benton-Banai, available from the Red School House, 643 Virginia St., St. Paul, MN 55103.

Ti-Jean and the White Cat - FRENCH CANADA

This story was collected by Marius Barbeau from the teller Achille Fournier and published in "Contes Populaires Canadiens," *Journal of American Folk-lore,* vol. 19, 1916, pp. 45-49. In translating it into English I tried to keep the same pace as the original French but occasionally I made minor changes so as to make the action clearer.

Brer Rabbit and the Rock Soup - AFRICAN AMERICAN

This tale was adapted from the text in *Negro Myths from the Georgia Coast Told in the Vernacular,* collected by Charles C. Jones (1888). You might wish to tell a number of other stories with this motif, so that you can compare the different ways in which people responded to such a trick. Marcia Brown's *Stone Soup* (c. 1947) is set in Europe in the time of Napoleon. Other stories like it can be traced by using the *Storyteller's Sourcebook* compiled by Margaret Read McDonald (1982).

The Little Red House - UNITED STATES

This story is reprinted, with minor adaptations, from the version first published in *Stories for Sunday Telling* by Carolyn Sherwin Bailey (1916). I have tried in vain to locate other versions in folktale collections, but a number of books on European folk customs related to plants cite the custom of cutting the apple in this way, so as to show the star. In some cases, this custom was attached to Christmas celebrations. In Christmas week 1972, while visiting a convent of the Daughters of Charity in Krakow, Poland, with my two sisters, we were served the most delicious apples I have ever tasted. One of our Polish hostesses cut the apples crosswise, showed us the star, and then peeled the apples and gave us pieces, all the while chattering away in Polish. I realized later (to my great chagrin, long after I returned to New York), that she was telling us a story about the star in the apple.

America South of the Rio Grande

Juan Tonto - MEXICO

This tale is translated, and slightly adapted, from Howard T. Wheeler's *Tales from Jalisco Mexico*. The tales were collected in the 1930s and published as Memoirs of the American Folklore Society, no. 35, 1943. When telling this riddle story, I generally ask the audience if they can guess what Juan Tonto's explanation will be. With a few hints, they can usually figure out all of the things, even the head lice! Because head lice have become such a common health problem in schools today, I thought it was a good idea to add the part about the bath.

Gammon and the Woman's Tongue Tree - JAMAICA

This story was reprinted from the *Jamaica Journal*, vol. 17, no. 1, 1987. It won a gold medal in the Jamaica Festival of the Arts. Diane Brown was born in Kingston and still lives there. She is married, has two daughters, and is an editor in a publishing house. Used by permission of the author.

Casi Lampu'a Lentemue - PUERTO RICO

Pura Belpre mentions, in the introduction to her book *The Tiger and the Rabbit* (Lippincott, c. 1944) that she learned most of her stories from her grandmother, when she was growing up in Puerto Rico. Because I was lucky enough to work with Ms. Belpre in the New York Public Library for a number of years, I had the opportunity to hear her tell many of her stories. The told versions were always a bit different from those versions she had written down. Best of all, she taught me the tunes to some of the little songs that appear throughout her tales. The song for this story appears in *A World of Children's Songs*. This story is, of course, a variant of "Rumpelstiltskin" and "Tom Tit Tot." Whenever children would ask what *Casi Lampu'a Lentemue* means, Ms. Belpre would always talk about magical power and mystery, but she would never give a direct answer.

Yes or No - BOLIVIA

Gaby de Bolivar lives in Cochabamba, Bolivia, and is active in trying to get books and materials published for all of the children in her country. This story is well suited for a program on International Children's Book Day, April 2. Used by permission of the author.

The Singing Frog - ARGENTINA, VENEZUELA

This is my retelling based on two oral versions I heard performed by tellers in the *Taller de Narracion* directed by Juana La Rosa, Buenos Aires, Argentina, and at a storytelling workshop in Banco del Libro, Caracas, Venezuela. I often tell this bilingually, using felt figures for each of the characters. For those who want a text in Spanish, one of the better versions can be found in *Folklore para Jugar* (Editorial Plus Ultra, 1987, distributed in the United States by Bilingual Publications, 270 Lafayette, New York, NY 10012). There are many other good versions available in Spanish, but I know of no others in English translation. The Mexican version, words and music, can be found in *Spanish-American Folk-songs* collected by Eleanor Hague, published as *Memoirs of the American Folklore Society*, no. 10, 1917. Hague's English translation and the music are in *A World of Children's Songs*, a companion volume to this one.

Oceania

I Am Forgiven - MALAYSIA

This story is adapted from a story in *Interlit*, David C. Cook Publishers, Elgin, Ill., March 1992. Ms. Tinggal is a new writer. This is her first published story.

To start a discussion after reading this story, try asking questions such as these: Do you think it was fear of her father that forced the girl to take action or her own inner sense of right and wrong? What do you think of Mr. Oldie's treatment of the children he catches stealing?

The Story of Our Fingers - PHILIPPINES

Both the rhyme and story were collected by Dean Fansler in the first decades of the 20th century. They were among the many tales he wrote down in *Filipino Popular Tales*, published as *Memoirs of the American Folklore Society*, vol. 12, 1921.

How the Land Snail Got His Shell - FIJI

This story was reprinted from *Coconut* (vol. 2, no. 1, no date). *Coconut* was a children's magazine published by Lotu Pasifika, Suva, Fiji, for a number of years. Unfortunately, it is no longer available.

Index by Title

Index by Country and Subject